Euphoria

Book Boyfriend Series #3

Erin Noelle

Never Stop Flying xoxo Erin Noelle

Euphoria

Published by Erin Noelle

Cover Photo by: Toski Covey Photography ~ Custom Designs

Cover Graphics & Design: by Hang Le

As a part of the Book Boyfriend Series, numerous characters from other books are mentioned throughout the text. The following is a list of said characters, the books you can find them in, and the author who owns the characters and titles. The author highly encourages the reader to read all of the mentioned books so that one can better understand the context in which it is used.

Emerge ~ S. E. Hall

Hopeless ~ Colleen Hoover

Game of Thrones ~ George Martin

Remy ~ Katy Evans

Knight & Play/ Knight & Stay ~ Kitty French

The Avoiding Series ~ K.A. Linde

Fallen Too Far Series ~ Abbi Glines

The Mighty Storm/ Wethering the Storm ~ Samantha Towle

When It Rains ~ Lisa De Jong

For Carly Simon ~ I bet you think this book is about you

PROLOGUE ~ Christmas Night
Reminder ~ Mumford & Sons
Lips of an Angel ~ Hinder

ASH

Frustrated. That summed up my mood in one word. I was frustrated with Scarlett for bailing on our Christmas dinner, really frustrated with my sister for standing up for her, and extremely fucking frustrated with Mason for being such a stupid ass to get himself in this mess. If I didn't know better, I would've thought he did it on purpose just to see if she would come running to him. Which of course she did. Fucking always. I'm not a violent person, but I really wanted to beat the shit out of someone that night. It was a good thing that he was in a different state 'cause if he had been close, I may have finished the job for him.

The frustration was eating me from the inside out as I sat alone in my house after the awkward holiday dinner with my family. My mom hadn't said much except that she understood why Scarlett left. Will commented that the situation was jacked up, which led to Crys getting mad at him and telling him he was insensitive ass. He shut up shortly after that. Oscar and Evan were oblivious to it all ~ they ate as quickly as possible so that they could get back to playing the Xbox. I sat silently eating the food that she and I had prepared the night before, trying not to think of the reminder fuck I had given her at the kitchen sink. Obviously it wasn't a reminder enough.

I decided I needed to do something except lie in bed alone thinking about what could possibly be happening in Florida. The frustration was quickly turning into anger and I needed to cool off. I got up and threw on some jeans and a long sleeved Henley, ran my fingers through my hair, and slipped my feet in some flip flops. Grabbing my keys, wallet, and phone, I called Nicholas as I headed out to my car.

Five minutes later I was pulling up to his house, and it appeared I wasn't the only person looking for a place to hang out for the evening. The driveway and street were packed with cars and the music was flowing from the house. The scene reminded of the many Saturday nights that I had spent there~ drinking, playing the guitar, and hooking up with random girls. It also reminded me of the first night I met Scarlett. Fuck, I couldn't escape thinking about her. I shook my head at my pathetic self as I walked up to the front door. I needed a drink... or twelve.

As I made my way through the living room to the kitchen, I spotted Nicholas and Jess standing at the island and headed in their direction. We exchanged hugs and wished each other Merry Christmas before Jess asked where Scarlett was. I knew it was coming, but I really just didn't want to talk about it.

"Something came up," I answered vaguely. "Now where's the whiskey? I need a shot stat."

Jess raised her eyebrows at me and was about to say something else, but Nicholas whispered something in her ear and she closed her mouth. He gave me a knowing look and I made a mental note to thank him later.

"The liquor's at the bar and the beer's in the fridge dude. Help yourself. It's good seeing you here; we've missed you coming around," he replied.

"Thanks man."

"You gonna play tonight for us?"

I hadn't really thought about it, but now that he mentioned it, it sounded like a great idea. Music was always a good prescription for the soul.

"Yeah, I think I will. Let me get my buzz on and I'll grab your guitar."

Three shots and two beers later, I was sitting on the back deck, acoustic in hand with most of the house guests sitting around me. I loved winter nights in Houston. It never got that cold, the air had just enough chill in it to make you feel alive. Couples were cuddled up watching the flame inside the chimenea and a flicker of jealousy shot through me. Scarlett should have been there with me, not sitting next to Mason's hospital bed taking care of him.

I took a long gulp of my beer and settled the guitar in my lap. I went through my usual favorites, a little Jack Johnson, Ben Harper, and such, before taking requests from people. After a couple of more songs, a familiar-looking blonde girl that had been trying to catch my eye all night asked me to play *Lips of an Angel*. Not thinking much about it, I began playing the popular Hinder song, but by the time I finished the end of the first chorus I thought I was going to be sick. It wasn't that the song's lyrics really applied to my life or situation exactly, it was just the subject matter of cheating and the fact that I kept having to saying the word *Angel*. Knowing that's what Rat called Scarlett, I could totally picture him singing it to her and I suddenly despised the song that I had never given a second thought to. As soon as I spat out the last verse, I abruptly rose to my feet, setting the guitar in my chair, and claimed I needed a drink break.

I walked back in the house to escape everyone for a minute, especially Blondie who had kept inching closer to me throughout the song, and I poured another shot. Throwing the glass back, the warm liquid tingled my throat and chest as it settled in my gut. After repeating the motion two more times, I heard the back door open and close and I assumed Jess had come in to ask me what my problem was and where Scarlett was exactly. I closed my eyes and grabbed the counter to steady myself in the somewhat blurry room. However, the hands that wrapped themselves around my waist from behind and the voice that whispered in my ear didn't belong to Jess.

"My lips are soft as an angel's... especially when they're wrapped around your cock. Don't you remember, Ash?"

Oh fuck.

CHAPTER ONE
Stubborn Love ~ The Lumineers
I Try ~ Macy Gray

MASON

Her voice was the first thing I remembered hearing as I pulled through the fogginess that weighed heavy on me physically and mentally. I could hear the determination in every word and the resolve in each strum of the guitar as she sang to me about keeping me alive and not allowing me to escape. She still loved me. I knew she still fucking loved me. I slowly opened my groggy lids and focused on the beautiful image that sat next to my bed, completely oblivious to where we were or why we were there. All I cared about was that Scarlett was sitting next to me.

As she finished the song, she opened her dampened brown eyes and looked down at me. The look of relief and sheer joy that spread across her face when she saw me staring back at her filled me with a happiness that I hadn't felt in a long time... since the day she had walked back into Empty's after being gone for eight months.

"Am I in heaven now, Angel?"

My voice was raspy and strained but my words were clear. She reached out and brushed the pad of her thumb across my cheek, and even though I loved the feel of her skin on mine, I hated the pity in her eyes.

"Mase, baby, what have you done?" She whispered as the tears began steadily rolling down her cheeks.

I grabbed the wrist of her lingering hand and brought it to my mouth, kissing her fingertips. She quickly stood up, placing the guitar in the chair she had been sitting in, and crawled into the bed next to me. It was until that moment that I wondered why the fuck I was in a hospital bed. Looking around, I realized that I wasn't just in a hospital bed, I was in an actual hospital with all kinds of wires and tubes and shit hooked up to me.

Weakly, I pulled her close to my body, and she cautiously cuddled up to me with her head on my chest. Unable to resist, I lowered my face to her hair, inhaling deeply, and gently kissing the top of her head. The longer I was awake, the more my body began to throb with pain, but I didn't dare say a word about being uncomfortable. I would've laid on burning coals if it meant I could have Scarlett in bed with me. Neither of us said a word for several minutes. I wasn't sure what in the hell she was thinking, I knew whatever I had done had upset her, but for the life of me, I couldn't remember anything past getting ready for a Christmas Eve party.

"Scarlett?" I croaked. "Can you tell me where in the hell I am and how in the fuck I got here?"

She twisted her body so that she was looking up at me, and I desperately tried not to wince, but gauging from her reaction, I failed miserably.

"Oh, I'm so sorry," she said as she attempted to gingerly move away from me, but I wrapped my arms around her and held her close to my body.

"Shh. Don't you dare go anywhere and don't apologize either. I need you next to me."

She relaxed back against me but kept her eyes locked on mine. "You really don't remember what happened?"

I shook my head and closed my eyes, trying again to recall the events that had led me to being there. I knew it must've been serious if Scarlett was sitting at my bedside playing music asking me to fight for my life, but I really had no idea.

"You overdosed, Mason. On Christmas Eve night at some party here in Miami. I'm not sure what all you were on, but from the contents of your hotel room, I have a pretty good idea." Her voice quickly changed from caring and concerned to disappointed laced with disgust. I groaned as her words cut into me, I was ashamed and embarrassed.

Just as I was about to apologize and ask her why and how she had gotten there, the door to my private room flew open and my older brother, Marcus, came barging in with a nurse hot on his trail.

"You stupid, selfish, fucking little prick!" he roared. "What in God's name are you doing? Have you lost your fucking mind? You finally get a shot... a chance to make a name for yourself... to get your sorry ass out of Houston... and this is what you do?!?"

He looked down at Scarlett who was still lying in the bed with me. "And what the fuck is she doing here? Hasn't she done enough?"

"Shut the fuck up Marcus! Don't talk to her like that!" I glared at him. "You don't know what you're talking about."

The nurse finally broke in, "Gentleman, you are going to have to keep your voices down. There are other patients in this hospital that are trying to rest and this language will not be tolerated," she said sternly. Turning to look at Scarlett, "And you need to get out of that bed young lady; this isn't a hotel. You should've come to get someone as soon as he woke up."

I continued to hold Scarlett close to me, despite her attempts to wiggle out of my arms. I didn't want either my brother or Nazi nurse to intimidate her, and the last thing I wanted was her away from me. And if the scene wasn't chaotic enough with Marcus standing at the foot of the bed with steam coming out of his ears, the nurse looking back and forth between all of us with a massive scowl on her face, and me having to borderline wrestle Scarlett to keep her in the bed, the door opened and yet another person joined the party.

Walking through the doorway, Smiley, my manager Jag's girlfriend, took a few steps into the room and then stopped as everyone's attention turned to her.

"Hullo, I umm, just dropped by to see how Rat was feeling," she said in a thick British accent as she tucked a long strand of dark brown hair behind her ear. She looked around my brother's large frame and made eye contact with me as a huge smile lit up her face. "Oh good, you're awake. I'm so happy to see you're doing better."

Scarlett's body tensed next to me at the sight of a young, very attractive girl coming to check on me, which made me happy. Like I said, she still loved me. Marcus smirked thinking that some hook-up of mine had stopped by, which he assumed would cause an issue with the girl in my arms. And the nurse rolled her eyes and sighed aloud.

"Hey, thanks for coming by," I greeted her. "Yeah, I just got up a bit ago; you've made it just in time for the celebration. I hope you brought a twelve pack."

Rolling her eyes playfully, she walked up to the bed and patted my calf. "Jag will be thrilled to hear that not only are you alive, but you haven't lost your cheeky arse attitude either." Stretching her hand out towards Scarlett, she introduced herself, "Hi, I'm Smiley, Jag's girlfriend and unofficial tour bus mother."

Relaxing, no longer seeing her as a threat, Scarlett returned the smile and the handshake and said, "Scarlett and it's a pleasure to meet you. I understand we have you to thank for finding Mase the other night. I can't even begin to express my gratitude."

"Not necessary. I'm just glad that we got him to the hospital before anything serious happened. We all care about each other quite a bit, we're like a family. " She turned her dazzling smile and outstretched hand towards Marcus. "Speaking of family, the resemblance is undeniable. You must be Rat's brother. It's very nice to meet you as well."

Before he could respond, Nazi nurse had decided that was enough pleasantries and interrupted the introductions. "I'm going to get the doctor for an evaluation. You will all need to leave the room when he gets here." She turned her nose up at all of us and marched out the door.

The moments of silence that filled the room after was moderately awkward, and then everyone tried to speak at once.

"I'm gonna grab a cup of coffee."

"I need to go to the ladies room."

"I'm going to call Jag and give him an update."

"I'm ready to get back to the bus."

After my comment, the three of them all turned and looked at me like I had grown a second head. "What?" I asked. "I need to get back to the guys, we leave for Europe soon."

Smiley cocked her head and said sweetly, "Rat, the tour is over for you babe. You've got to go back to Texas and get help. I'm sorry."

"Are you serious?!" I asked, raising my voice. I was so pissed. What did they mean I couldn't finish the tour? I was fucking fine. I had a bad night; it wouldn't happen again. What the fuck?

Not fazed by my yelling in the least, her smile never wavering, she nodded her head. "I'm afraid so. We can't take you in your physical or psychological state overseas. Despite the health issues, you are a tabloid story waiting to happen. We can't take that risk."

Not wanting to believe the words that had just left her mouth, I screamed at her, "Get the fuck out of my room! Now! You don't know what the fuck you are talking about! Who do you think you are, you uppity British bitch?! Get Jag on the phone. Now."

The smile finally drained from her face as she did an about-face and walked out of the room without saying another word. Good, I was tired of her happy ass face all the time anyway and that stupid ass nickname. Marcus shook his head at me and mumbled something under his breath before following her. Fuck him too. Fuck everybody. Now that Scarlett was back in my arms, I didn't need their shit.

Just then, the doctor entered the room and Scarlett quickly crawled out of the bed, straightening her clothes as she stood up. Walking towards the door, she looked back at me right before she left and said, "It's gonna be okay, Mase. I promise."

SCARLETT

My back hit the wall in the hallway outside Mase's hospital room and I slowly slid down until my butt met the floor. I pulled my knees to my chest and buried my face in my arms, trying to pull myself together. Completely drowning in a flood of emotions, I could hardly think straight. First and foremost, I was relieved that he was awake and appeared to be physically okay. I knew he was a long way from being *fine*, but at least he was going to be around for us to work on that. After relief, I couldn't say what I felt more ~ frustration that he had been so reckless and selfish in his decision-making and actions, guilt knowing that I had been one of the main factors for leading him to this point, exasperation that he actually thought he could go back on tour without getting any help and with the way he had spoken to Smiley, comfort by the way his arms felt around me, and love ~ I'd always love him. Even if I knew we couldn't be together in a romantic sort of way, he would always own a piece of my heart.

A few minutes after I sat down, I heard footsteps approach me followed by someone joining me on the floor. I looked up to see Smiley sitting to my right, an understanding look on her face.

"You doing okay, sweetie?" she asked.

I was so exhausted I didn't even care that she called me sweetie. It actually felt kind of nice. I shrugged. "I guess. I'm just..." My voice trailed off.

She reached over and pulled me into a hug, patting my hair. For some reason, it didn't feel strange at all. Typically, I wouldn't be too keen on letting a stranger hold me and comfort me, but it was exactly what I needed at that moment. Neither of us said anything, we just sat there on the floor hugging. Hospitals make people do weird shit.

"I see you two have met," Cruz's voice pulled us from our embrace. I looked up at him standing over us with a smirk on his face, a tray of coffees in his hand.

"Hey you. Join us and give me one of those," I said tugging on his pant leg.

Careful not to spill the hot liquid, he knelt down next to us and passed us each a cup. Smiley looked down at the drink and made a funny face.

"What?" He asked her. "I brought cream and sugar if you don't want it black."

"I just don't usually drink coffee, I'm more of a tea girl," she retorted. "But I suppose that's probably not an option here."

Cruz rolled his eyes and I giggled. "You fucking Brits and your damn tea. Drink your coffee and shush," he joked.

We were all laughing hard as the doctor exited the room and walked over to us. Scrambling to our feet to hear what he had to say, I was quickly reminded why we were all there and the seriousness of the situation.

"It appears your friend is going to be just fine if he can lose the 'I'm invincible' attitude," he said. "I'd like to keep him one more night just to monitor his vitals and do some more blood work, but assuming everything looks okay, he'll be released tomorrow morning." He turned to walk off, but stopped after a few steps and looked back at us. "If you don't want him back here or in some other hospital, possibly with a worse outcome, someone needs to make sure he gets help." He then continued down the hall and out of sight.

The three of us stood there looking at each other, not knowing what to say or who should go in and talk to him. Taking a deep breath, I said, "I'll tell him. I'll take him back to Houston and between Marcus and myself, we will make sure he gets clean so that he can rejoin the band as soon as possible."

"That sounds good," Smiley agreed. "I know he doesn't want to see or talk to me right now, and I get it. I'll let Jag know."

"Yeah, I'll let the guys know too. We're bummed about not finishing the tour, but we know that we need to fix this problem now. Not to mention, Sebastian needs a bit of an intervention as well, so hopefully Aaron, Sophie, and I can work on that," Cruz added.

"Okay then, wish me luck," I said as I kissed his cheek and gave her a quick hug before walking back into Mase's room. "I'll talk to y'all back at the hotel in a bit."

As I pushed the door open, Mason was already out of bed changing into his clothes. He looked up at me with those piercing grey eyes and smiled. "Let's get out of here, Angel."

CHAPTER TWO
Bulletproofangel ~ Goo Goo Dolls
I Won't Let Go ~ Rascal Flatts

MASON
As soon as Doctor Dickhead left the room, I pulled the monitors from my chest and the IV out of my arm, which hurt like a bitch by the way, and got out of the bed. I wasn't staying in that place another fucking minute; they couldn't legally keep me there. I found some of my clothes folded on a chair by the window, so I quickly stripped out of the hospital gown and began putting my jeans on. As Scarlett walked through the door, the surprise on her face was evident as she saw me up and getting dressed.

"Let's get out of here, Angel." I said with a smile. I knew she was about to try to talk me out of discharging myself, but I wasn't changing my mind. I was fine, and I had shit I needed to take care of. Laid up in a hospital bed for another night wasn't going to solve anything.

"Mase, the doctor just told us that you need to stay another night for them to monitor you. Why are you getting dressed?" she asked concerned.

"I'm good, Angel. I need to get shit sorted out and I can't do that lying in a damn hospital bed. I feel fine," I said as I pulled the t-shirt over my head.

I walked over to where she was standing, still close to the door, and cupped her beautiful face in my hands. I tilted her chin up and locked my eyes on hers which were still moist from crying earlier. I wanted to kiss her sweet full lips more than anything in the world, but I didn't want to push my luck. She was there with me, even though it apparently took me nearly dying to get her there, but I didn't want to drive her away. Everything felt okay when she was around, it always had. She unknowingly gave me strength through her presence, and despite her flaws, she was still so much better than I could ever be. Since she had been out on her own, life hadn't been easy for her, and I knew that I had played a part in messing up shit for her. I should've been upfront with her about wanting her to move with me to Austin. If I hadn't been such a fucking pussy, none of that shit with Bentley would've ever happened nor anything that happened after. Despite all of that, there she was, by my side when I needed her. My bulletproof angel.

"You promised me everything was gonna be okay before you left the room, and now I'm promising you that I'm fine to leave. I really need to get out of here. Please don't fight me on this." My thumb stroked back and forth along her cheek bone, and she nodded apprehensively. I kissed her forehead and then grabbed her hand to pull her out of the room.

A heated confrontation with the charge nurse and thirty minutes later, Scarlett and I were in a taxi heading back to the hotel. She hadn't said much of anything since we had left the room. There was so much I wanted to ask her, but I wasn't really sure I wanted to know the answers. *Who had called her? How long had she been there? Where was emo-boy? What did he say about her coming? What did this mean for us now?* I decided there would be plenty of time for talking later, I was still feeling extremely sluggish, even though I wouldn't admit it, and judging by the dark circles under her eyes, she looked like she needed some serious rest too. So instead of saying anything, I just held her hand tightly in mine until we reached the Bentley. Worst fucking hotel name ever.

Cruz was sitting with Marcus and Jag at the bar in the lobby when we walked in. As soon as he saw us, I heard him curse and jump off his bar stool as he headed towards us.

"Dude, what the fuck are you doing here?" He asked before looking at Scarlett. "Did you not hear the doctor? He was supposed to stay until tomorrow."

"It wasn't her's or the doctor's decision to make. I'm fine and I didn't want to be there any longer," I answered sternly before she had a chance to say anything. "

"Rat, you almost died. You were unconscious for over a day, and you've only been up for a couple of hours. I hardly think you're *fine*," he hissed.

By this time my brother and manager had joined us and they both added their support of Cruz's assessment of the situation. Scarlett, still silent, squeezed my hand hard as I addressed all of them. "I had a bad fucking night, okay? It won't happen again. I don't need to spend another night in the hospital for them to tell me I need to chill on partying. I got it. Now we're gonna go to my room and get some rest. I'll be ready to leave tomorrow morning. Excuse us."

I pulled Scarlett by the hand, bumping Marcus' shoulder with mine as I passed by him.

"The tour is over for Jobu's Rum," Jag's voice stopped me mid-stride.

Turning around abruptly, I pleaded, "I said I will be okay, man. I really need to finish this." Cutting the tour short was not only devastating to me, but to my best friends and band mates. I didn't want this to be over for any of us.

"Mason, you've still got a bright future ahead of you. Jobu's Rum has been a huge success so far. We can put together something for you in a few months, once you get some help, but you need to go home and get your shit together."

I knew by the tone in his voice and his body language that he wasn't budging on this. Defeated, I turned back around and continued on to the elevator. I hated everyone in that moment. Everyone but Scarlett.

Once we were in the room, all I wanted to do was take a shower and go to sleep. I didn't want to think about anything or anyone.

"I'm gonna take a shower, Angel, then get some rest. I'm fucking exhausted and I'm in an awful mood."

"We need to talk Mase," she answered meekly.

Running my hands through my grown out hair, I sighed loudly. "I know we do, Scarlett. Apparently I'm gonna have a lot of free time in the next few months to talk, so we can do it later. Okay?"

She took a deep breath, and I could see her trying to muster up the courage for whatever she was about to say. "No, it's not okay. You're not *okay*, and you aren't *fine*. You need help. I'm not gonna sit around and watch you destroy yourself. Things will never same between us, Mase. We can never go back to where we were, but I'm not gonna turn my back on you when you need someone to love and support you. I'm sorry for what I did to you... to us." She paused and looked down at the ground for a moment, shame washing over her face. Raising her chestnut eyes back to mine, she continued, "I won't fail you. I promise I won't let you fall again."

SCARLETT

Once Mason had showered and fallen asleep, I grabbed a room key and quietly let myself out the door, heading back to the tattoo shop I had sat in front of the previous day. An hour and a half later, I was walking back to the hotel smiling for the first time since I had landed in Miami. I absolutely loved my new ink ~ a permanent reminder that I needed to fly with my own wings, that I could never truly be happy until I learned to love myself for being just me. I still had a long way to go to get to that point, but I had finally realized that not Ash, Mason, nor Max... no anyone else could do that for me.

Mason was still asleep when I returned to the hotel room, in the exact position that I had left him in. Sitting next to him on the bed, I gently stroked my fingers across his cheek. He looked so vulnerable in that moment, any negative thought that I had ever had about him, was washed away as the love I still had for him flowed freely. I was so worried about him; I knew that he should've stayed in the hospital one more night, but damn if he wasn't the most stubborn person I had ever met. I could only hope that he would seriously try to get help and get his life cleaned up. I would do everything in my power to make sure that that happened. I just wasn't sure how Ash was going to feel about it...

Completely exhausted myself from the events of the previous twenty four hours, I moved to the other side of the bed and lied down next to him. My shoulder was a little tender from the tattoo, but I wasn't awake long enough to care. Seconds after my head hit the pillow, sleep consumed me.

I had no idea what time it was when I woke up. The room was dark and there was no sunlight shining through the window; the only way I could see anything was from the faint glow of the streetlights outside. Despite my lack of vision, my sense of touch was definitely working, and there was no doubt that kisses were being peppered on the inside of my thigh, moving right up to the most sensitive spot on my body.

CHAPTER THREE
Come Home ~ One Republic
Chasing Pavements ~ Adele

ASH

The day after Christmas was always one of my favorite days of the year ~ that was until that year. I woke up with a pounding headache, a stomach begging to be purged, and the worst case of cotton mouth ever, but none of those things compared to the awful empty feeling I had inside ever since Scarlett had left the day before. The attempt to drink my woes away at Nicholas' house only led to more problems as the girl from the night of Evie's funeral attempted to seduce me in the kitchen. Thankfully Jess walked in just at that time to save me. And by save me, I mean she kicked the girl out and told her she wasn't welcome at the house ever again. There was no way in hell that I would've touched her, or anyone else for that matter, regardless of how much I had to drink, but Jess taking care of it for me made it much less awkward.

I stumbled into the bathroom and stared at my reflection. I looked nearly as bad as I felt with dark circles under my eyes and stringy, oily hair plastered to my face. After brushing my teeth, I took a long shower trying to wash the funk off, but that unsettling feeling still sat heavy in my stomach even after I was clean and dressed. I didn't want to spend the day moping around the house thinking about what she was doing, so I called Max to see if he had plans.

An hour later, as I sat playing Xbox with him, I realized that hanging out at the apartment he shared with Scarlett wasn't doing much to help me not think about her. Everywhere I looked I saw something of hers, and it took everything in me not to go lay in her bed just to feel closer to her. I was losing my mind wondering what was going on in Miami, and if I was honest with myself, I knew that I was petrified that I was going to lose her to him again. I hadn't heard from her since her plane landed the previous night, and I had refrained from calling to get a status update. And by status update, I meant when she was coming home... as long as Rat was simply alive, I could really care a less about his ass.

The longer I sat there, the more that stomach-turning feeling of something not being right continued to eat at me. I knew it wasn't just the remnants of the hangover, it was a real gut check.

Abruptly, I dropped the controller on the couch next to me and jumped up.

"I'm going to get her," I blurted out.

"What? What do you mean?" Max asked, looking up at me like I had lost my mind.

"I'm not going to let him weasel his way back in. I finally got her back, and I'll be damned if I lose her again," I explained. "I'm going to claim what's mine."

"Well, I'm going with you then," he replied as he stood up next to me. "I've got a bad feeling about this."

I didn't answer him because honestly, I had a bad feeling about it too. Instead I waited silently as he threw some clothes in a duffel bag and checked the apartment to make sure all the lights and electronics were off. We stopped off at my house for me to do the same before heading off to the airport. Once we got there, I realized that I had no idea when the next flight was or anything else. It took a little bit of time for us to get the tickets purchased, and then even longer to wait for our flight, but finally at six thirty in the evening, we were airborne and I was on my way to get my butterfly.

It was late on the east coast when our plane touched down, and I was completely exhausted by the time we got to the hotel. I decided to wait until the morning to call Scarlett in case she was already in bed. I assumed she was most likely drained, both physically and emotionally, from the events over the past few days, Plus, I had no idea what hotel she was even in.

That night I got the worst sleep ever. I tossed and turned with visions of Scarlett and Mason together running on loop through my mind. I had never been so happy to hear the alarm clock go off at seven o'clock. I knew it was early, but I couldn't wait another minute to hear her voice. I grabbed my phone and hit the first name listed in my favorites.

"Hello?" a sleepy male voice answered.

With that one word, my world came crashing down around me as I realized that my worst fears had come true.

SCARLETT

"Scarlett, wake up," I heard Mason's voice say as he shook my shoulder. "Scarlett... Scarlett, get up now. Ash just called your phone."

Hearing Ash's name, I sat up instantly and looked around trying to get my bearings. I realized I was on the couch in the living area of the hotel suite, and the events of the previous evening flooded my memory.

Waking up to kisses on my inner thigh, I moaned slightly and leaned my head back in to the pillow. My legs instinctively had spread open to make room for him to settle between my thighs, and within seconds my body was aching in anticipation for his mouth to land on my mound. Keeping my eyes closed, not wanting to end this dream-like state, I lifted my hips slightly and moved my hands into his hair to hurry along the tortuous process. As my fingers slid through the short locks, it was then that I realized that it wasn't Ash in bed with me. My eyes flew open as I cried, "Stop! Please stop!"

"Scarlett, you need to call him back," Mason's voice pulled me from my reminiscent thoughts. "I didn't even realize it was your phone on the table and I answered it. He didn't say anything... just hung up..."

I snatched the phone from his hands and immediately called him back. My body was shaking with panic; I could only imagine what Ash had thought when Mason answered my phone so early in the morning. Silently praying for his understanding as the phone rang, I was relieved that he answered and didn't completely ignore me. I needed to explain everything quickly.

"Ash, thank God," I said as soon as he picked up. "I can explain."

"That's really not necessary, Scarlett," he replied icily. "I heard what I needed to."

"It's not what you think..." I tried to clarify as the tears began rolling down my cheeks. "My phone was in his room, I wasn't. I promise."

"Whatever, Scarlett. I'm just going to go back home; I don't know why I even came here in the first place. I guess I just needed to confirm what I already knew."

"What did you just say? You're gonna go home? You're here?" I asked completely confused.

I heard him sigh dejectedly on the other end of the phone before he answered. "Yes, Max and I came last night. I hadn't heard from you and I thought you may need the support."

If I didn't already love him so incredibly much, I would've fallen head over heels for him in that moment. He had come all the way to Florida to be there for me, knowing that I was most likely an emotional mess over my ex-boyfriend's overdose.

"Ash, I swear to you, nothing happened. Mase checked himself out of the hospital yesterday. I must've sat my phone down by the bed when I was helping him get settled. I slept on the couch... I promise I'm telling you the truth," I pled through my sobs. At some point during the conversation, Mason had gone back into the bedroom, and I was thankful for the privacy.

We both sat there on the phone quietly for what seemed like forever. I didn't know what else to say; I needed so badly for him to believe me. After all we had been through, I didn't want to lose him over a misunderstanding.

Finally, his voice broke the silence, "Okay, I believe you. As hard as it is for me, I'm trusting you; please don't let me down."

A huge weight was lifted off my chest with his words, and I needed to see him immediately. "Where are you at?" I asked.

"We are at some hotel by the airport... I'm not even sure. It was so late when we got in last night, we just stopped at the first place we saw. Where are you?"

"We are at the Bentley Hotel."

Even Ash couldn't help but laugh at the irony of the name. "Are you serious? Who booked that place?"

Chuckling, I replied, "Yeah, pretty awesome, right?"

"Yes, very. Ok, well I'm gonna assume that Rat is fine since he is out of the hospital, so Max and I are coming to get you, Butterfly. We'll be there in just a bit, wait for us in the lobby, okay?"

Even though it gutted me to leave Mason so soon, I needed to reassure Ash that he was who I was in love with and wanted to be with; there was no way I was arguing with him. After all he was right- Mase was fine; he had people there to take care of him and to make sure that he got back home okay. I needed to take care of myself and the functioning relationships I still had. I knocked on the bedroom door and despondent grey eyes greeted me.

"You don't need to say anything, Angel. I heard," he mumbles.

Seeing him like this was almost as heartbreaking as seeing him lying half dead in the hospital bed, completely dejected and crestfallen. I brought my hand to his cheek and my thumb caressed back and forth over his smooth skin. He closed his eyes and pressed his palm against my palm. Once again, tears streamed down my face as my heart broke for him... for me... for the us that could've been.

He opened his eyes and leaned forward until his forehead was pressed against mine. Staring deep into my eyes, he whispered, "Please don't go, Angel. We can make this work, I know we can."

His combination of his promising words, the look of determination of his face, and the feel of his breath on my lips was almost enough to convince me that he was right... almost. I inhaled a deep breath before speaking. "Mase, so much has happened between us. We can't just pretend that it hasn't. We can never get back to where we were."

"We can be better than we were, Scarlett. Please just give me a chance."

I brushed away the wetness from his cheekbone and I placed my finger over his lips as he was about to say something else. "I can't Mase. I love you, but I just can't. Please understand."

Afraid that if he said anything else, I would break down and tell him that I would stay with him and give us a chance, I turned on my heel, grabbed my bag, and walked into the hotel hallway. Just before the door closed behind me, I heard him say, "I will never stop loving you, Angel."

I made it to the elevator before I completely broke down sobbing. Leaning against the wall, I let it all out, and I stayed there until I had no more tears left to cry. I then slipped into the bathroom and washed my face the best I could, but there was no getting rid of the puffy red eyes that stared back at me in the mirror. I took several deep breaths and did my best to regain my composure before heading downstairs.

Thirty minutes later I was standing in the extravagant lobby, my bag at my feet, waiting for Ash to get there. As soon as I saw his long blonde hair come through the main entrance, I took off running towards him. Nearly tackling him to the floor, I jumped on him and began kissing him all over his face. Laughing and squeezing me tightly, I knew he felt the same relief and comfort that I did being back in his arms. I saw Max standing a few feet away, giving us our space, he had a huge smile plastered on his face. I grinned back, thanking him silently for his support. Despite the numerous bumps and detours of the previous year and a half, I felt that I had finally found the path I was supposed to be on to find my happiness.

CHAPTER FOUR

She is Love ~ Parachute
When the Lights Go Down ~ Jason Walker

ASH

Seeing Scarlett's face light up when she saw me caused my heart to swell until I thought it was going to burst. I had told her on the phone that I believed her, and I did for the most part, but her reaction to my arrival in the hotel lobby gave me the reassurance that I needed. After our somewhat obnoxious public display of affection, which I could've given two shits about, Max, Scarlett, and I headed straight to the airport. I wanted to get her as far away from him as soon as possible.

As we waited for our flight, we grabbed some food and drinks in one of the airport restaurants. I didn't care that it was nine o' clock in the morning, I needed a drink. I had been a tightly bundled ball of nerves for two days, and I finally felt that I could relax a bit. Max and I both had a couple Bloody Mary's with our breakfast as she nursed her milk and sugar with a dash of coffee. It was in that moment I was reminded of how young Scarlett still was. Still just nineteen, out of her parents' iron-clad restraints for only a year and a half, she had dealt with a lot in that short amount of time. Even though I was only three years older and had dealt with my fair share of life's disappointments and misfortunes, just as everyone does, most people are taught to deal and cope with these things beginning at a young age. Her parents had really done a disservice to her keeping her sheltered from the reality of the world.

"Is your drink really that interesting?" Scarlett's voice broke through my thoughts. My eyes snapped up to hers and she had this cute little smirk on her face. "You've been staring at it and stirring it with that celery stalk for the better part of five minutes while Max and I have been arguing if window or aisle seats are better. We really need you to be the tie breaker on this one, if we can tear you away from your precious Mary."

I snickered as I looked back down at my drink and saw that my hand was still swirling the green stalk in a circular motion. Quickly pulling it away and grabbing the glass, I took a long drink before pushing my serious thoughts from my mind and enjoying the company of my two closest friends.

"Well, there really is no argument. The window seat is by far the more superior of the seats on a plane," I said matter-of-factly.

"How can you say that?" she exclaimed. "If you have an aisle seat, you don't have squeeze past anyone when you need to get up for the bathroom, you don't feel claustrophobic being squeezed between two people or a person and a wall, and most importantly, if there's a need for evacuation, you're the first to get your ass to the exit doors." Max rolled his eyes, as she had apparently already spouted off these reasons to him.

"Scarlett, honey," I began, knowing how much she hated to be called *honey*. I couldn't help but laugh as she wrinkled up her nose at the word, giving me exactly the reaction I knew she would have. "If you have a window seat, no one squeezes over you to go to the bathroom... no one's ass is in your face; it's your ass in someone else's face, so who cares. Secondly, you don't feel claustrophobic at all because you can look out the window!! And to your last point, I don't get on a plane thinking about the possibility of a crash. If a tin can is going to fall out of the sky and land either in water or on land, I don't think chances of survival are very good no matter what seat I'm in. In addition to all of that, the window seat gives you the luxury of seeing and connecting to the beautiful earth below you. Have you ever flown into a big city like New York or Vegas late at night and seen the lights from the plane window? Or ever looked down as you fly over a large body of water and thought about the expansive marine wildlife that is below you? Or ever wonder how so much of the land seems to be divided into perfect squares? Or..."

"Okay, okay!! You win, the window seat is the best," she interrupted, rolling her eyes.

Max started cracking up laughing at her obvious attempt at agreeing just to get me to shut up. "Well done, man. She's one stubborn little bratty flamingo."

Scarlett couldn't help but giggle at his ridiculous flamingo comment as she punched him in his arm. "And just for all that, I'm sitting by the window on the way home. You two can fight over middle and aisle."

We spent the next hour continuing the light-hearted conversation, none of us wanting to venture into the topic of why we were all there. I knew that she and I still needed to have a very serious conversation, but it wasn't the time or place to do it. For the moment, I just wanted to enjoy the smiles and laughter.

SCARLETT

From the time Ash had picked me up at the hotel, he had not stopped touching me. He was either holding my hand or had his hand on my leg or his hand at the base of my back... some sort of physical contact at all times. It was almost as if subconsciously he needed to feel me to remind himself that I was there with him. And even though I loved how it made me feel cherished, it also made me sad that he was that insecure in our relationship. I knew it was my fault that he felt that way, and I knew that it was my job to fix it. We still had a lot to talk about; I needed to be honest about the lingering feelings I had about Mase, and also express to him the difference in my love for the two of them. However, at the end of the day, words were just that... words. They meant nothing without the actions to back them up. It was time to show Ash Walker that he was who I wanted in my life.

Once we landed in Houston, Ash drove Max and me to our apartment. As we approached the complex, an uncomfortable silence fell over us. I wasn't sure if he wanted to go home or to stay with me, to talk or not talk. I kept waiting for him to make some reference to what he was planning on doing, but instead he just clammed up. I figured that was a good of time as any to start showing him how I felt, even if I was moderately scared of rejection.

He pulled the car into a parking spot and Max jumped out of the back seat, escaping the evident awkwardness. "I'd really like if you'd stay with me tonight," I said quietly, staying in the passenger seat.

He turned to look at me, his blue eyes bright and hopeful. "Are you sure? I didn't know if you needed some time alone or... whatever," he replied as he ran his fingers nervously through his hair.

I shook my head no. "I never want to be without you, Ash, especially not tonight."

He didn't wait another second. Smiling, he turned the key, killing the engine, and hopped out of the car. He raced around the front of the car to my door, where he opened it and in a silly accent said, "Madame, please allow me to escort you into your estate."

I threw my head back in laughter at his antics, but placed my hand in his allowing him to help me from the car. Upon entering the apartment, Max was nowhere to be seen so I assumed he was hiding in his room, and quite honestly, I couldn't blame him. He and I really needed to have a Chocolate Bar session soon, but there was only one thing on my mind at that moment.

Ash and I headed straight for my bedroom, and closed the door behind us. Wasting no time, I slipped my shoes off and pulled my shirt over my head. He stood there staring at me, and I wasn't sure if he was just watching me or was uncertain about what exactly I had in mind. I walked up to him, standing in my bra and jeans, and grabbed the hem of his shirt and raised it up and over his head. Once he was shirtless, a mischievous grin spread across his face and he reached down to unbutton and unzip my jeans. Biting my lip as the anticipation began to grow inside of me, I followed suit and unfastened his belt and pants, never once tearing our gaze from one another's. He kicked of his shoes and allowed his pants to fall to the floor, then stepped out of them, as I shimmied out of mine.

We stood there nearly naked for several minutes, never speaking a word, but saying so much to one another. Finally, he brought his hands up to cup my face and leaned down until his face was so close to mine that I could feel his breath on my lips. "I'm so glad you're home, Butterfly," he whispered, ever so softly. Then he pressed his lips to mine, firmly and with purpose, taking control of my entire body and soul.

Quickly we stripped out of the minimal clothing we still had on, and found our way into my bed. Beginning with my mouth, Ash took his time kissing every inch of my body. His tender lips caressed my delicate skin as I melted into a pool of lust under this lean, muscular frame. The minute his mouth hit my throbbing clit, I could no longer control myself. As good as it felt when he licked and sucked on me, I needed to feel him inside me. My whimpering turned into begging as I tugged on his hair. "Ash... please... you... me... inside... now." Those were the only words I could manage to form in between the moans that kept escaping my lips.

Needing to feel me as badly as I needed him, he didn't torture me long. Moments later he slid his way back up my body until he was eye level with me. Hovering over me, the warmth of his love filling my heart, he brushed a strand of my hair off of my face and tucked it behind my ear as he lowered his mouth to mine. Gently, he pulled my bottom lip in between his, sucking slightly, at the same time that he slid his hard cock into my drenched slit satisfying the ache deep inside me.

Completely captivated by the passion, it didn't take me long to reach my peak and to take the ecstasy-filled tumble down. Feeling and hearing my orgasm sent Ash over the edge right behind me. My walls clenched tight around him as I felt his body go rigid and then as he released himself inside of me. He collapsed on top of me, gasping for breath, as I locked my arms and legs tightly around his body holding him close. We were a mess of sweaty perfection, and I was glad to be home.

CHAPTER FIVE
Stay Close, Don't Go ~ Secondhand Serenade
Three Little Birds ~ Bob Marley
The Last Time ~ Taylor Swift/ Gary Lightbody

MASON

Watching Scarlett walk out of my hotel suite was even harder than watching her leave me at the wedding. At the wedding I had been angry and raw, a bit out of control, but in the hotel I was just completely devastated. I walked back into the bedroom and sat down on the bed, lost in what to do next. The previous couple of months my life had gone to shit. Ever since I had moved to Austin, in what was supposed to be my huge step towards the life I had always wanted, everything had just fallen apart. I had lost sight of the things that were supposed to be important in my life ~ Scarlett, my music, and my brother, and traded them in for cheap fixes in alcohol, drugs, and groupies. I had apparently almost died, but I honestly didn't feel any different physically just days later, so I wasn't convinced it was as serious as they had all made it out to be. The worst part of it all was thinking that Scarlett had come back, that we were going to give it another shot, only to be shattered when she walked away again.

I understood what she said about so much happening between us, but I didn't agree that it was more than we could handle. I was willing to forgive her for all that she had done wrong, but seemingly she couldn't do the same. I believed that she loved me; regardless of her fuck ups, her heart was pure and her intentions were good. I always knew that Ash had some sort of hold on her, but I had truly believed that our love was true and we could overcome that. Obviously I had been wrong.

Sighing, I looked at the side of the bed that she had laid on the night before, where for a few short minutes I had tasted her sweet flesh against my lips once again. I didn't want to accept that it would be the last time I would hold her so intimately, despite the reality that it most likely was. I had wanted so badly to go after her, to beg her one last time, but in spite of my complete mental and physical breakdown, I still held some semblance of pride. A few minutes after she left, I thought I heard crying in the hallway, but I resisted the urge to see if it was her. It absolutely killed me to see her cry, even knowing that it was her decision to walk away, I still hated that she was distraught.

A knock on my door pulled me from my depressing thoughts. Both Marcus and Cruz were standing there with concerned looks on their face as I threw the door open.

"Come on in to the suite of despair," I said with a forced laugh. I motioned them in with my hand and walked towards the kitchenette. "Can I grab y'all a drink?"

I reached for the bottle of Jack Daniels and three rocks glasses without waiting for an answer. I poured three double shots and slid them each a glass.

"No," Marcus said firmly as he slammed his hand on the countertop.

I looked up at him confused. "No? What's your deal, dude? You've been nothing but a dick since you've gotten here."

"Are you serious, Rat? I just flew halfway across the country, on Christmas no less, to see my baby brother lying in a coma in a hospital bed because he overdosed!! And you're going to ask me what my fucking problem is?!" His face was beet red as he lectured me. "You really need to take a step back and reevaluate your situation. You've had your head so far up that girl's ass you don't know what the hell's going on. Ever since she came into your life you've completely lost all sense of reality. And yet today she has fucked you over once again because here you sit wallowing in your sorrows while she just skipped out of the lobby kissing emo boy."

"Shut up! Just shut the fuck up!!" I screamed at him. "Ever since the day she walked into Empty's, my life has finally made sense. I was doing all this shit before she was around and none of you seemed to care then... She makes me want to be a better person; can't you see that?"

He slid the still full glass back towards me and turned around to leave. "You need help little brother," he said as he walked to the door. "And I hate to break it to you, but your precious little angel can't fix this. As a matter of fact, she's really no angel at all."

I looked up at Cruz who had been silent throughout. I was so livid I could barely speak. I assumed it was his turn to pile on, but instead he just followed Marcus out the door without saying a word.

I looked down at the three glasses in front of me. I knew I had a problem, I knew I needed to push them away, but I couldn't do it alone. A mixture of emotions coursed through my body- rage, despair, sadness, frustration, and most of all loneliness. There I stood all alone, and yet once again, my old friend Jack was there to pick me up. I hurriedly downed all three drinks, allowing the warmth of the whiskey to flow freely through my veins and numb the cold, empty feeling away.

As I slammed the final glass onto the countertop, I mumbled to myself, "She is too an angel. She's my angel."

SCARLETT

Ash and I spent the rest of the afternoon and night in my bed, only getting up to use the bathroom and get food. We made love several times around watching some old movies, but neither of us ventured into deep conversation. Several times I found myself wondering how Mase was doing or when he was coming home, but each time that I did, I consciously pulled my thoughts back to my surroundings. I didn't think that Ash noticed anything wrong or off, but each time my mind began to wander, I would curl up into Ash and kiss him to remind me of why I'd made the decision I had.

The next morning I awoke early as the sun came streaming through the window. I tried lying there, willing myself back to sleep, but to no avail. I decided to get up and cook breakfast for the boys... a little way of showing gratitude for them coming to get me. I threw on some yoga pants and a thermal top, put my ear buds in, and quietly made my way to the kitchen.

My cooking skills were mediocre at best, but breakfast was something that I could actually do which was most likely why Max and I ate breakfast for dinner pretty regularly. Luckily we had all of the ingredients for what I wanted to prepare, and after I got out all of the bowls and skillets that I needed, I got right to work.

I put my iPod on random and allowed the tunes to set the pace for my cooking. Bob Marley's unmistakable voice was the first to flow through my speakers, and I couldn't help but dance around with a goofy grin on my face as his infectious lyrics reminded me to not worry because every little thing was going to be alright. I quickly lost myself in the task at hand, cracking open eggs and frying up bacon, while I tried to stay somewhat quiet as Ash and Max continued to sleep. I was getting close to finishing everything when a song came on that I didn't even realize I had in my music library. About halfway through it, I stopped and looked at my phone to see who and what it was ~ The Last Time by Taylor Swift and Gary Lightbody. I restarted it so that I could really focus on the lyrics, and I couldn't help but think how relevant it was to mine and Ash's situation, except I should've been singing the guy's part. I realized that this really was the last time he was going to take me back if I walked away from him or put someone else in front of him, this was the last time I had to prove to him that I

26

chose him. I had to figure out a way to get over Mase, and focus on Ash. When I sat down and thought about it logically, there really never was a choice. I knew from the moment I laid eyes on Ash that he was destined to be in my life. Even if I didn't believe in fate and all of that, Ash had so much to offer me. He was incredibly smart and working towards a promising career in astrophysics, he was unarguably good looking, we had common interests in music and art, and most importantly, he was in love with me and treated me like the most precious thing in the world. He was undoubtedly the most logical choice, the only problem was convincing the part of my heart that still loved Mase of that.

I was so lost in thought that I didn't even hear Ash get up and join me in the kitchen. He slid his arms around my waist from behind as I stood at the stovetop, and then softly kissed his way up my neck to my earlobe as he greeted me.

"Good."

Kiss.

"Morning."

Kiss.

"Beautiful."

Kiss.

"Butterfly."

He then pulled my lobe in between his lips and sucked lightly and nipped at it with his teeth. I closed my eyes and moaned in delight, forgetting the internal debate I'd been having just minutes before.

"Morning yourself, sleepyhead," I said teasingly, as I spun around in his arms.

"Sleepyhead? It's not even eight o'clock in the morning," he retorted as he kissed the tip of my nose. "You should still be in bed."

"I couldn't sleep any longer so I thought I'd make breakfast."

He chuckled as he looked around the kitchen at all of the pots and pans and the sink full of dishes. "Breakfast or a feast? Who are you expecting? The entire Texans football team?" He grabbed a piece of bacon from the cooling rack and shoved it in his mouth.

"No, I just couldn't decide what to make so I made everything," I explained.

"What's this about the a Texans football team?" Max asked groggily as he emerged from his room with his hair sticking up and out in every possible direction. "And what smells so good?"

"Morning Max. It's probably the disappearing bacon," I said cheerfully, swatting at Ash's hand as he stole himself a second piece and one for Max too.

"You two sit down and I'll bring everything to the table," I instructed them. Obligingly, they both plopped themselves down in the dining room chairs and waited for me to serve them.

Twenty minutes later we had all stuffed ourselves with ham and cheese omelets, French toast, hash browns, sausage, and of course, bacon. We all sat there for several minutes silently, in food-induced comas. I looked back and forth between Ash and Max's smiling faces and felt grateful to be sitting there with them after everything that had happened. Finally Max stood up, looked at Ash, and asked, "Is it too early to kill people?"

Laughing and shaking his head, Ash replied, "It's never too early to kill people." He turned to me and asked, "Do you mind if I play for a bit? I'll help you clean up in a little while."

I glanced at the kitchen and groaned; it looked like a bomb had gone off in there. I didn't feel like tackling it just then anyhow. I smiled brightly at him and said, "Nah, go ahead. I'll make us all some fresh coffee and then I'll read a little. We can clean later."

After brewing a fresh pot of coffee and taking the guys their cups, I curled up on the couch next to Ash and dove into *Emerge* and followed Laney Walker in her search for love. Little did I know how much I would connect with her as first Evan, and then Dane, stole my heart like they did hers. At sixty six percent, I had to put the book down. My stomach was tied in knots and I thought I was going to be sick. Any progress that was made, as little as it may have been, in regards to me forgetting Mase had been demolished. Laney couldn't have summed it up any better than when she thought "absence makes the head dizzy and fills the heart with aching bewilderment." My head felt like I had just gotten off the spinning Mad Tea Cups and my heart was being tossed around in the darkness of Space Mountain.

I sat my kindle down on the couch and excused myself to take a shower, giving Ash a quick kiss before leaving the room. I needed to pull myself together and get a grip on reality. Standing in the bathroom, staring at myself in the mirror, I reminded myself, "This is the last time, Scarlett. Don't tempt fate."

CHAPTER SIX
Leader of the Broken Hearts ~ Papa Roach
Where Are You Now ~ Mumford & Sons

MASON

Three days after I checked myself out of the hospital, I found myself on a plane heading back to Houston... alone once again. Marcus had left Miami the same day that he had stormed out of my hotel room. He had sent a text on his way to the airport saying that since I was obviously fine and didn't need his help or advice, that he needed to get back to Empty's. As my only living relative, and for as close as we once were, I thought it was pretty shitty of him to leave that way, but I wasn't really surprised. I was quite used to being deserted by those who supposedly cared about me.

Cruz had called me to let me know that the rest of Jobu's Rum had gone back to Austin to play some smaller local gigs while I went to rehab. Even though I knew I had a problem, I didn't really think it was necessary for me to check in to a live-in assistance center, but Jag didn't give me much of an option. He had told me that if I wanted to stay on as a client of the Donovan Group and have any chance of touring with VanderBlue again, that I would spend six weeks in house at The Right Step center and then another four to six of outpatient care. He required that I be sober for twelve weeks before he would even think about booking another show for me.

Groaning to myself as I thought about the upcoming three months of hell, I leaned back in my seat as the plane began to taxi down the runway. As much as I tried to not think about her, it seemed I couldn't go more than about five minutes without wondering where Scarlett was at that moment or what she was doing. Unfortunately, those thoughts normally ended up with me envisioning her lying in Ash's arms which sent a surge of pure envy through me. I had no idea how to even begin getting over her, especially if I had to do it sober. I wasn't sure how much I would see her once I was back in Houston, if she would come visit me at the center, or if she was just done with me entirely. My chest physically hurt at the thought of never seeing her again. Despite everything, she still owned me, body and soul, and unfortunately, she didn't want either.

An hour later as the flight attendant sauntered down the aisle with the drink cart, I didn't even think twice about ordering the whiskey from her. After all, it was my last few hours of freedom before I would be basically put in prison, so I might as well enjoy and live up to the addict that everyone made me out to be. I handed her my credit card in return for the tiny bottle of liquid gold, and I laughed aloud at the size of it.

"What's the maximum number of these I can buy at one time?" I asked her in all seriousness.

Apparently it was three, so I of course bought three. I drank them all straight from the bottle, not even bothering with the glass of ice she had sat on my tray table. As I guzzled them in three gulps, I heard someone snicker from across the aisle. I turned my head to see who found my antics so amusing, and surprisingly found myself looking in the eyes of an attractive woman, who I guessed to be in her early thirties.

"Are we celebrating or forgetting?" she asked in a sultry voice, as she shamelessly looked up and down my body.

I smirked at her, attracted by her boldness. "Oh, we are definitely forgetting," I answered. "Unfortunately, there's not enough alcohol on the planet to make me forget completely."

She twisted her body in her seat so that she was better facing me, and not coincidentally, giving me a better view of her amazing rack. She uncrossed and recrossed her legs which drew my gaze down to her toned calves and thighs that were on display, barely covered by a black suit skirt. My pants instantly felt tighter as my cock swelled while I took her in. She didn't say anything for a few minutes, allowing me to enjoy the view, and as my eyes travelled back up her body and met hers again, she grinned knowingly and unapologetically.

"Sometimes forgetting isn't the answer, Hun. If you forget completely, then the lesson that was to be learned is lost and the pain and heartache were for nothing," she said matter-of-factly. I didn't respond immediately, as I let her words sink in.

"By the way, my name is Heather," she continued, as she offered me her hand. "I apologize if I've over stepped, but I'm not one to sugar coat situations, and you look like you've been through Hell recently."

I took her dainty hand in mind and shook it. "I'm Mason, it's nice to meet you Heather. And you have no idea... as a matter of fact, I'm pretty sure I'm still there," I replied with a chuckle.

She nodded her head understandingly and looked at the empty bottles in front of me. "Well only you can get yourself out of there, and I hate to break it to you, but those are only gonna make you sink further down." She exhaled loudly as she turned to face the seat in front of her, and mumbled under her breath, "Believe me, I know."

I got the feeling that she didn't want to further discuss her last comment, so I changed the subject to why she had been in Florida. Over the following hour we discussed the pros and cons of warm weather and cold weather vacations, and then listed all of the places that we wanted to visit in our lifetime. It was nice to not think about anything serious for a little bit, and once I got over my initial reaction to her attractiveness, I found it refreshing to have a conversation with a beautiful woman that wasn't sexually stimulated. Maybe I wasn't as big of a douche as I thought I had become.

The end of the flight came quickly and after collecting our luggage at the baggage claim area, I thanked Heather for the company and wished her well. As I watched her walk away, appreciating her long legs once more, after all I was a red blooded male and you would have to have been blind to not notice, I realized that I would probably never see her again in my life, but her words about making the hurt worth it and not forgetting the lesson learned would stay with me forever. Unfortunately, I was still searching for the lesson in the midst of all of the anguish and despair that I had endured over the past couple of months.

Shaking my head as I cleared my thoughts, I slung my bag over my shoulder and walked outside in the crisp, clear night to grab a taxi. I wasn't due to check myself in to the rehab clinic until early the following morning, but I knew that going to my empty apartment would only bring back memories of Scarlett and the short time that she and I lived there together. The last time I had been there was the morning that I had returned to tell her that I couldn't live without her and to ask her to move to Austin with me... the morning that I found her and all of her things gone for good.

I gave the driver the address for the center knowing that if I spent one more night alone, I would just end up, at minimum, drinking my sorrows away. Chances were I'd also find someone to keep me company and I'd end up regretting my actions in the morning, just like I did with all of the others. No matter how much I drank or what drugs I smoked, snorted, or swallowed, they weren't my angel and all paled in comparison. Thirty minutes later, the car pulled up in front of the white building that I would call home for the following forty two days. I paid the driver, grabbed my bag, and slowly made my way through the front doors.

The woman sitting behind the main desk looked up and smiled brightly as I entered the lobby area hesitantly.

"Good evening! Can I help you sir?" she asked cheerfully.

Taking a deep breath, I acknowledged the multitude of emotions running through me, primarily fear and anxiety but a sliver of hope kept one foot moving in front of the other until I was standing directly in front of her.

"Hi, I'm Mason Templeton, and I'm here to learn my lesson."

SCARLETT

Two and a half weeks. It had been seventeen days since I had walked out of Mase's hotel room and I had heard nothing from him or his friends, I had absolutely no contact. I was about to lose my mind if I didn't find out where he was or at least find out if he was okay. After the conversation in the hospital room, I knew that Marcus didn't care for me, which was putting it lightly, so I really didn't want to call him to get an update. Truth be told, he'd probably cuss me out and hang up the phone on me. I had refrained from contacting Cruz because... well, I really didn't know why. I guessed I just kept hoping that Mase would call me and let me know what was going on, but I had finally accepted that wasn't going to happen. I wasn't sure if I should take that as he didn't want to talk to me or if he thought I didn't want to talk to him. I absolutely hated not knowing.

In addition, Ash and I had still not talked about the entire Miami fiasco. We had come back home and just swept the entire event under the rug, pretended that it never happened. Things were good between us, we were getting along great, but Mase's name was never brought up. I had tried several times to begin the conversation, but I always chickened out because I hated thinking about causing issues between us when things were going so smoothly.

The day classes resumed for the spring semester, I saw Mina walking in the courtyard in between my first two classes. It was the first time I had seen her since the wedding and we greeted each other like long lost friends that hadn't seen each other in year, not just weeks, as we squealed, hugged, and jumped around. Some of the passersby looked at us like we were crazy, but I didn't care one bit. She was the only girl friend that I had in my life, and with all of the drama that had happened, I was ecstatic to see her.

"Scarlett! Oh my God! I've missed you!" She shrieked as her blonde curls bounced up and down when she hugged me.

I squeezed her tightly to my body and mirrored her excitement. "I know!! I'm so happy to see you! When did y'all get back from your honeymoon?" I knew that she and Noah were going to Telluride for snow skiing but didn't know for how long. I was still kind of in shock that she was actually married.

"We've been back for about a week, just lying low, relaxing at the apartment. What about you? I heard there was some excitement with Mason at the reception, but I was so busy with the wedding stuff that I never heard the true story about what happened."

My stomach turned nauseous at just the thought of that night and the things that were said and done outside that tent. I really didn't want to discuss it again, but knew that Mina deserved to know what had happened with everything since that night. "Come on lets grab a coffee and I'll give you the Cliff's Notes version of the last few weeks of the soap opera that is my life."

As we walked to the Starbucks on campus, I caught her up with everything from the moment that Mase had shown up to her wedding and sang *I Love You* to me up until that moment in time that I had still had no idea what was going on with him.

"Oh my word. I can't believe that Scar. That's just terrible; I can't believe he OD'd," she said shaking her head. "We had no idea of any of that. I'm surprised that Max didn't call Noah to fill him in. I'm just in shock."

"Yeah, it's all been pretty crazy," I replied meekly. "I just wish I knew where he was right now. I know I need to leave him alone... for the sake of mine and Ash's relationship, but I want to know that he's okay and getting help, ya know?"

She stared at me with a serious look on her face and asked, "Is that all you really want, Scarlett? That would make you happy?"

I nodded in response as I approached the barista and ordered us both a venti caramel macchiato. "Yes, I care about him as a person, and I'd like to know that he's getting his shit together."

She didn't say anything, but instead pulled her phone out of her purse and began to make a call. I raised my eyebrows at her, questioning what she was doing, but she just held one finger up in the air at me, indicating that I needed to wait. A few moments later, a smile spread across her face and she greeted the person on the other end of line.

"Hey Cruz, it's Mina. How are you?" She paused as he spoke. God, I hated only hearing one end of a conversation.

"I'm good, thanks, and I will pass on your regards to Noah. Hey, I heard what happened in Miami with Mason and I was just calling to get an update on him. "

"Oh, he is? Well, that's good."

"Yeah, I know he is."

"Where?"

"Okay cool, sorry for calling so early and waking you up. I appreciate the info."

"Yep, you too. Bye."

She hung up the phone and I anxiously awaited the news that she had been informed of. "Well..."

"He's in drug and alcohol rehab at a place called The Right Step here in Houston," she said softly. "Cruz says he seems to be doing really well but has a few more weeks of staying there before he's released."

My brain started moving a thousand miles an hour at the news of where he was and what he was doing there. An internal battle that I had struggled to keep dormant for several weeks instantly became front and center.

"Scarlett, you said you just needed to know that he was okay," Mina's voice startled me. "Don't make any brash decisions. It's obvious that you still have feelings for him, but I don't want to see you throw away anything that you and Ash have built for something that can never be."

I smiled at her, hoping it didn't appear as fake as it felt. "I know, Mina. I appreciate you calling Cruz to find out for me. I do feel much better now."

We separated for our next classes a few minutes later and made plans to have dinner the following Friday. Throughout my English Lit class the following hour, all I could do was think about Mase in rehab. I had so many questions... so many things to say to him... Halfway through the lecture, I succumbed to the temptation and pulled out my phone and googled the facility. I found out the visiting hours as well as jotted down the address. I managed to wait until the class was over before running to my car and hitting the highway. The entire drive to the center I toyed with whether or not I should call Ash and tell him where I was going. I ultimately decided that it was one of those better to ask for forgiveness things than ask for permission, so I opted not to. A little less than an hour later, I pulled into one of the visitor parking spots and walked to the front door. My heart was pounding nervously inside my chest as I had no idea of what he would say when he saw me, but regardless of what his reaction would be, I had to see him again.

After I signed in with the office, I was led to a common room where I was asked to wait. It seemed like forever that I sat there, looking around at the other patients talking to their visitors, some conversations appeared to be happy and uplifting while others seemed tense and uneasy. Then from behind where I was sitting, the voice that I hadn't heard in seventeen long days serenaded my ears with just one word.

"Angel."

CHAPTER SEVEN
Demons ~ Imagine Dragons
Wherever You Will Go ~ The Calling

MASON

I had been in rehab for just a couple of weeks, and surprisingly, it had been much better than I thought it would be. As I sat in my bed, I thought back to the day that I had begun that next chapter in my life ~ sobriety.

The night I had checked myself in, I was shown around the facility and then taken to the room that would be my only personal space for the foreseeable future. My room was small and simple, just enough room for a single bed, a small dresser, and a desk. Everything was white- the furniture, the linens, everything. The place was much nicer than I had originally expected, but it was still a rehab facility ~ still a place where a bunch of people who were fucked in the head were all corralled into one enclosed space. The following day, which was my first full day there, I was taken to meet my assigned therapist first thing in the morning. As I sat in the chair waiting for the poor soul who had to try and figure out how to control my demons, I found that I was more nervous than I thought I would be. Knowing that you are about to be judged on all of the awful decisions that you've made is quite unsettling; I didn't want to be thought of as a bad person. I heard the door close behind me and the heels click on the floor as they approached the chair I was sitting in. You can only imagine my surprise when Heather, the woman from the plane, took a seat directly across from me dressed comfortably in jeans and a purple V-neck sweater.

"Mason?" She asked, appearing just as shocked as I was.

"Heather," I replied with a grin. Seriously, what were the odds?

"Well, this is quite a surprise, I must admit," she said, returning the smile. She held a file folder in her hand, but before opening it, she looked at me with her head cocked. "Before we get started, I'm going to give you the option if you'd like to be reassigned to a different counselor... seeing that we have met previously. It's vital in your recovery that you feel one hundred percent comfortable in this process."

I didn't have to think about it even for a minute. I wasn't thrilled to be in that place, but if I had to be, I might as well look at her pretty face every day. "I promise that I'm completely fine with you being my assigned counselor. Actually, I probably feel more at ease talking to you than some other stranger that's gonna tell me how I've fucked up my life. You've already told me that it's my fault I'm in Hell."

She leaned forward and lowered her voice, "Mason, I never said it was your fault. I'm not about placing blame or saying who or what is responsible for the place you are at in your life. It's my job to help you rectify the situation, and make sure that you don't get back there again. But like I told you yesterday, you have to want to get better. If that's not the case, then you are wasting everyone's time."

It was damn hard not to look down her sweater as she talked to me, but I refrained. For the first time that I can remember, I refrained. I figured I better take this shit seriously, otherwise I was never going to get a chance to play my music again. I had already lost Scarlett, so really all I had left was my music.

I looked into Heather's eyes and for the first time, I admitted aloud, "I want out of this Hell. I want to know how to cope with stress and anxiety without the aid of a drink or a joint. I want to be able to play my music and find happiness again. I want to learn how to live without her."

Fourteen days later, I was sitting in my bed with my guitar and my journal, furiously writing down the latest song that had taken my mind hostage, when one of the center's administrators, stuck her head in my room and announced, "Hey superstar, you've got a visitor."

Looking up at her, surprised, I asked, "Do you know who it is?"

"No, sorry, I didn't ask. I'm just relaying the message. I didn't even see them," she replied before walking on down the hallway.

I was a bit perplexed because I wasn't expecting anyone until the following weekend, when Marcus was supposed to stop by again. Since I had been admitted, I had had a total of three visitors, and to be quite honest, I really didn't feel like seeing anyone else. Marcus had come because well, he's my brother. No matter what happened between us, no matter what ugly things we said to each other, we were brothers forever. We always just wanted the best for each other. Cruz had come the first Sunday to bring me my guitar and to pass along well wishes from all the guys. I could tell that he was uncomfortable the entire time he was there, not that I could blame him much, so I told him that I greatly appreciated him coming to check on me and bringing me my instrument, but he really didn't need to make the trip again. I'd keep him updated with my progress via texts. The third and final visitor I had was Smiley, Jag's girlfriend and apparently, his assistant as well. If I used the word uncomfortable for Cruz's demeanor while there, I would have to say that she was downright petrified. By the look on her face, one would've thought she was going to visit a prisoner on death row. It pissed me off that Jag had sent her, that he couldn't be bothered with making the trip himself. I knew he had her come to make sure that I was doing what I was supposed to, but I was cordial to her and told her that she could report back that I was on my best behavior. I even apologized for my outburst towards her back in the hospital, in addition to thanking her for finding me that night at the party. Who knows what would've happened had I lain there unconscious much longer than I did. By the end of the visit, she had relaxed some but I still didn't think we were going to be BFFs any time soon.

Setting my guitar and notepad down on the sheets, I begrudgingly got up and headed to the activities room without even bothering to put any shoes on. Whoever was waiting for me was really interrupting my writing flow, and I certainly didn't feel like entertaining anyone. As I turned the corner and walked through the doorway, my eyes scanned the room looking for a familiar face. As soon as I saw the long, straight chestnut hair attached to the body that was undoubtedly Scarlett's, my heart stopped beating and I gasped for air. She had found me. Not only had she found me, but she had come to see me.

My first reaction was to run back to my room. I felt like I had made real progress in the couple of weeks that I had separated myself not only from the drinking and drugs, but from her. Heather had helped me realize that I had made Scarlett an addiction, just like the chemical dependencies, only she wasn't physically harmful to my body. It wasn't anything that Scarlett had done herself, it was the way I had deified her and put her on a pedestal. I knew that my love for her was true, but Heather had emphasized that because I didn't value nor love myself, our relationship had been doomed from the beginning. I was still working through a lot of these ideas and had finally begun to accept that I was worthy of someone like Scarlett, but that was without her sitting just mere feet in front of me. I was scared to death that if I stared in her big brown eyes, if I inhaled her sweet, heavenly scent, or if I touched her silky, soft skin, that I would fall right back into that unhealthy obsession I had for her, similar to the temptation of someone sitting a bottle of whiskey directly in front of me. That was the thing I had discovered about rehab right off the bat. It wasn't so hard to not drink or do drugs or any of the other bad shit while I was in there. It wasn't in thrown in my face, I didn't have to watch other people enjoy it while I abstained. The real test would be once I was back in the real world; the everyday life of a musician included witnessing many people partake in numerous gluttonous and addictive behaviors. I thought I had a couple more months of working on myself before faced with any of my vices; however, as I stood there struggling to breathe, the thing that I craved most in life had paid an early visit.

Vowing to not take the cowardly way out, to not run from my problems but to meet them head on, I walked over to wear she was sitting, stopping just a couple of inches behind her chair. I wasn't quite sure what to say to her. It was almost comical thinking about how natural talking to and flirting with girls had always come to me; I had never had to think about what I was going to say, I just said whatever the fuck I wanted to, and they all loved me just the same. However, in just two weeks' time, Heather had managed to strip me of pretty much every ounce of arrogance that I once had in abundance, while simultaneously trying to build my self-respect and worth. The first part had happened quickly, the second was a definite work in progress. Gathering my courage, I inhaled a deep breath and said the one word that came to my mind.

"Angel," I said as I exhaled.

SCARLETT

Frozen. I was frozen in my chair... afraid to turn around, afraid to look in those gray eyes that melt me every single time. The entire drive to the center I thought I had prepared myself for seeing him again, but the minute I heard his voice, I began having second thoughts about my unannounced appearance. Maybe I should've called first or maybe I should've just let things be, just knowing he was enrolled in a rehab program.

"Scarlett, turn around and look at me," Mason's gruff voice assaulted my ears.

Slowly, I stood up and turned around to look at where he was standing. My eyes instantly welled up with tears seeing him standing there barefoot in his baggy, tattered jeans and white undershirt. His dark brown hair was longer than I had ever seen it and it appeared he hadn't shaved since he had been there. His face had much more color than when I had last seen him in Miami and I could tell that he had put on a few pounds as well.

He held his arms open at me and I quickly closed the small gap between us, flying into his body, nearly knocking him over. His arms wrapped snugly around me and I clung to him as if my next breath depended on it. We just stood there holding each other for I'm not sure how long, my face buried in his neck.

"Angel," he repeated softly.

I pulled myself away from him so that my stare was locked on his grey, emotion-filled irises. "I hope it's okay that I came," I stammered.

"Of course it's okay that you came. I'm just shocked to see you; I didn't think you wanted to have anything else to do with me after..." his voice trailed off.

I grabbed his hand and walked us over to an empty sofa in the corner of the room. After we both sat down and made ourselves comfortable, not letting go of one another's hand, I brought my gaze back to his. "I told you that I'd always be here for you. Even if we aren't together in that sense, I will never abandon you, especially when you need support and a friend."

A small smile replaced the obvious tension in his face. "I'm sorry I didn't call. I wasn't quite sure what to say."

"It's okay, Mase. I understand. I'm just glad that you're here and getting help." I looked around the room curiously at the other people. "So what's it like? What do you do all day here?"

He chuckled. "It's actually not so bad. The first few days I was being my usual ass-ish self, but I've made a few friends now and it's getting better. I have an amazing therapist, her name is Heather and she's really helping me realize shit that I knew but didn't think much about."

I nodded and smiled brightly as he continued to talk about his previous two weeks, truly happy that he seemed to be making progress. After a little over two hours, one of the clinic's staff members came in the room and announced that visiting hours were ending and that we needed to wrap it up. I was disappointed that I had to go, but I knew that I needed to get home anyhow. I hadn't checked my phone the entire time I was there, and I was sure that Ash had most likely tried to contact me at some point.

We embraced each other tightly one last time before heading towards the door. As we got ready to go our separate ways, I wanted to ask if I could come back, but was scared he would say no. Almost as if he could read my thoughts, he asked, "Will you come back to see me again? I'd really like you to meet Heather. I've told her all about you."

Nodding emphatically, I replied, "Absolutely, Mase. Just let me know when and I'll be here."

"Okay, I'll text you later this week," he said as he turned around and walked in the opposite direction. I stood there watching him, feeling some relief knowing that I'd get to see him again soon. Once he was out of sight, I headed out the main entrance and to my car. Plopping myself into the driver's seat, I leaned my head on the steering wheel and wondered to myself what in the world I was going to tell Ash.

CHAPTER EIGHT
I Got You ~ Jack Johnson
Secret ~ Maroon Five

ASH

Life was good. I couldn't have been happier. I was beginning the last semester of classes for my Master's degree at St. Thomas, my family was more stable than it had ever been despite my parent's pending divorce, and mine and Scarlett's relationship couldn't have been going any better. It was almost eerily good; if I hadn't been such an optimist, I would've thought that I was being set up for major devastation.

I had promised myself to take things relatively slow with Scarlett, even though in my heart, I was ready to ask her to marry me at any time. I knew exactly what I wanted, and there was no doubt in my mind, she was it. However, I knew that she was still very young and inexperienced in relationships, so it was important that she felt comfortable and in control at all times. I wanted more than anything to move in with her, to spend most of our free time together, but I also recognized the importance of her learning that she was capable of living on her own, both physically and emotionally. Her parents had not allowed her to be independent at any point in her life, and even when she first came to college, she was extremely dependent on Evie. Of course this was why when Evie died, tragically and unexpectedly, Scarlett didn't know how to cope and she ran away. It was important to me that she learned, if ever anything happened to me or anyone else in her life that she cared about, that she would be okay on her own.

Once classes had gotten back in session in mid-January, Scarlett and I developed a routine that seemed to work perfect for both of us. Because we both had classes and work Monday through Thursday, we typically stayed at our own house those nights. We had tried studying together at the same house, and that always ended up with our books closed and our bodies naked. Unfortunately, neither of us were taking Anatomy and Physiology or Human Sexuality so we couldn't very well pass it off for research. We would text and talk on the phone throughout the day, but it still gave us time to be our own people. However, when Fridays would roll around, she was mine for the weekend. I drank in every minute I spent with her during those three days, and I made sure she knew exactly how special she was to me and how important she was in my life.

We never discussed Mason again after I had brought her home from Miami. I had no idea where he was or what was going on with him, and as far as I knew, neither did Scarlett. I could only hope that I never had to hear his name or see his face again in my life, but I doubted I would be so lucky. I knew that Scarlett had feelings for him, possibly even loved him, but as long as I kept her away from him and his toxicity, I had faith that our connection and love would trump any of that. Most importantly, I just needed to keep him out of her life.

Smiling as I sealed the envelopes on the completed transfer applications for the same universities on the west coast that I had applied to for my doctorate, I reassured myself that I was doing the right thing for Scarlett. She really needed a fresh start, away from everything and everyone.

SCARLETT

I continued to see Mason regularly at the rehab facility after my initial visit. The second time was the following Thursday, just two days later, and I was introduced to Heather at that time. When I first met her, I was intimidated to be quite honest. She was absolutely gorgeous with long, curly black hair, the most exquisite green eyes, and a figure to die for. She carried herself with a confidence that I'd never had, and I could see the way that Mason looked at her in admiration. I'd be lying if I said I wasn't a teensy bit jealous of her initially and was probably a bit standoffish, but once I started talking to her and got to know her personality, that envy quickly turned into respect and reverence. She was warm and personable, and it was obvious that she took her job very serious. She invited me to join Mason's therapy session the following Tuesday which I eagerly agreed to do. I was not only curious about how such sessions were structured and what they were like in general, but I was overjoyed to be a part of Mase's recovery and healing process. I still felt a huge amount of guilt and responsibility for his downward spiral and ultimately, what had happened to him on Christmas.

I was nervous the day that I arrived for the counseling, again just unsure of what to expect. Surprisingly, Heather's office was set up very similar to the activities room, just on a smaller scale. There was a comfortable couch and an oversized chair set up opposite of her desk and credenza. The walls were painted a rich yellow, almost a golden color, and there were numerous plants and abstract pieces of art scattered about the area. Overall, it was very inviting and uplifting and I could see how her patients would feel comfortable in there.

A few minutes after I was shown in, Mason walked through the door wearing his now signature jeans and white t-shirt. As soon as he saw me sitting there waiting, a huge smile stretched across his face and his eyes lit up. I jumped up and went to hug him, relieved that he seemed happy that I was there. We both settled on the couch and I was telling him about my classes that semester when Heather walked in. After greeting us and getting herself settled in her chair, she addressed us both.

"Mason and Scarlett, this is going to be a little different than my normal therapy sessions here at this facility, but I think that it's vital in both of you moving on with your lives and ensuring that those lives are prosperous and productive," she stated in a calm but serious tone. "Mason, as you know and as we have discussed at length, you have an extremely addictive personality. When most people hear the word 'addiction,' they associate it with something negative; however, there is a fine line between addiction and commitment . Where you should never let any one thing or even a couple of things dictate your life, being *devoted* or *dedicated* to something is a fabulous quality to possess. For example, being devoted to your significant other or your family, or being dedicated to working out or eating good foods, these things can lead to an overall healthy mental and physical well-being."

After a brief pause, she turned her attention to me, "Scarlett, I don't know much about your background other than the brief amount that Mason has told me. I know that you grew up in a different environment than most children, and I also know that you've dealt with losing someone that was very close to you not too long ago. I suspect in addition to those things, you feel a great deal of responsibility for what happened to Mason on Christmas and the events leading up to that night. Am I right?" I nodded in agreement, but did not say anything. She continued, "Scarlett, everything that happened to Mason is Mason's fault... his responsibility. He is an adult and has to be accountable for his decisions and actions. You can no longer carry around that guilt; you've got to let it go. Mason, tell her what you want her to know."

Mason turned to face me and reached for my hands, gently placing them in his before he began talking. "Angel, I owe you an apology. I'm sorry that I didn't handle things right in our relationship. From the very beginning, I always saw you as someone who was too good for me, someone I didn't deserve, and because of that I held back from you. It was like I was just waiting for it to fall apart, so I kept things from you. I should've told you about Bentley from the beginning, I should've asked you to come to Austin with me when I first moved there like I wanted to, and I should've made more of an effort to connect with you on a personal level rather than just a physical level. When Heather asked me to tell her about you, I realized that I actually knew so little. I couldn't even tell her what your favorite color is or if you had any brothers or sisters," he scoffed. "But I know that you shave instead of wax and which panties are your favorites."

I'm pretty sure my face turned fives shades of red before hitting deep crimson with that statement. I couldn't even look at Heather to see her reaction; I was even more mortified that it probably wasn't the first time that she had heard him say that.

He lightly brushed his thumb back and forth over the top of my hand. "I didn't say that to embarrass you; my point is that our relationship was primarily physical... at least on my end it was. Heather has explained to me love usually occurs in stages, and the first stage is infatuation. I'm not sure I ever made it out of this stage with you, and I'm sorry that I didn't allow our relationship to progress."

"It's okay, Mase," I interrupted. "I know that you didn't intentionally do that. And I know that I didn't always handle things the way I should have." I looked down at my lap as the memories of my night with Max flashed in my mind. "I'm sorry too. I shouldn't have believed Bentley; I knew that she was a manipulative and devious bitch. I should've talked to you before making assumptions and my own bad decisions."

Raising one hand up, he placed his fingers under my chin, forcing me to refocus my vision into his eyes. "Nobody's perfect, Scarlett. Not you... not me... no one. The decisions I made to lose myself in drugs, alcohol, and women after we broke up is not your fault. Yes, I was hurt, and yes, I was disappointed, but I made the choice to make a bad situation worse by getting involved in shit that I knew wasn't gonna do anything but bring me more misery in the long run. Okay?"

Again, I just nodded. I wasn't sure what to say really. I almost couldn't believe that it was my Mason sitting in front of me saying those things. I knew what he said was true, just like it wasn't Ash's fault that I ran away after Evie's death or Bentley's fault that I slept with Max. I made the choices to react in the manners in which I did; I failed myself in critical moments of which my character was tested.

Heather's voice pulled me from my wandering thoughts. "Scarlett, why did you come here to see Mason last week?"

I looked up at her, a bit befuddled. "Because I love him, because I care about him. I needed to see with my own eyes that he was here getting the help that he needed."

"Not because you felt guilty or felt pity?" she asked.

"No," I answered ardently. "I'm not saying that I don't feel guilt because I do... or I have, but I would've come to see him no matter the reason or circumstances that he was here. And I've never felt pity towards him. I may not understand the things he does, but never pity."

She looked at Mason, "I'm very proud of you today, Mason. I know saying a lot of that wasn't easy, but it needed to be said for both yours and Scarlett's sake. Now the last thing that needs to be discussed is where each of you see your relationship going in the future, if anywhere. If you both to choose that today is the last time you see one another, I feel confident that you can both put the past behind you. You've both apologized to one another, and you both seem to understand that it's time to take responsibility for yourself and your own decisions. Many people are dealt really shitty hands in life, but there comes a time that you have to forget the past and take control of your future. Remember, in the end, it's not about where you start, it's about where you finish."

Heather leaned back in her chair, and crossed her hands in her lap. She looked at me, then at Mason, and then back at me. "So the future... Scarlett, look at Mason and tell him how you see y'all's relationship going forward."

I slowly shifted my weight so that I was turned towards him. I took a moment before saying anything, as I gathered my feelings and thought about exactly what I wanted to say. "Mase, I can't say what will happen or not happen in the future, but for now I want to be your friend. I want to get to know you, the inner you. I'm not sure what stage or what kind of love I have for you, but I know that I do love you. I care about you tremendously and I want you to be happy. I'm with Ash, and he makes me happy. He and I do have a connection on a cerebral level that you and I never reached. Mentally and emotionally, he's there for me." It took everything in me to not start crying while I said that, but somehow I made it through with dry eyes.

Not breaking our stare, he took his turn. "I'd be lying if I said that I didn't want to try again with our relationship, to start over knowing what we know now, but I realize that isn't what's supposed to happen right now. I would love to be your friend. I would love to know what your favorite color is and if you have any siblings. I want you to be happy, and if Ash makes you happy, I'm okay with that. I know that I have a lot of work still to do on myself before I can even think about focusing my attention on someone else."

We sat there for several minutes after he finished talking just smiling at each other. I honestly felt like we were going to be okay, both individually and together as friends. Heather offered one last piece of advice before excusing us both from her office.

"Many psychologists refer to euphoria as a state of intense happiness and self-confidence, a blissful self-clarity if you will, and most people throughout their lives search and strive for this feeling. Why many never achieve it is because they never learn how to love themselves. When you discover the true beauty of self-love, then and only then, will you experience pure euphoria. Today you both took a step in the right direction in your quest; don't look back now."

Mason and I walked out of her office hand in hand and headed towards the activities room. Neither of us mentioned what was talked about in the session for the rest of the afternoon, but I could feel the positive energy radiating from both of us. We attempted to play chess, but neither of us really knew all of the rules, so it ended with us both in a fit of laughter, and then spent the remainder of the time talking about our favorite books. Since he had quite a bit of free time in the center, he had been reading quite a bit over the prior few weeks, and I loved seeing the enthusiasm in his face as he talked about some of the journeys he had been on with the written word. It was no secret that I was a reading nut, so being able to share that exhilaration with him was awesome. We each agreed to read one of the other's favorites over the next week even though our genres of choice were quite different. I downloaded Hopeless by Colleen Hoover on his e-reader for him and it appeared I was going to begin the Game of Thrones series. I didn't care that I wasn't a fan of supernatural type books, if he liked it so much, I was happy to give it a try.

Before I was ready, it was time for me to head to work, and I hugged him like I had the previous couple of times that I had visited, but this one felt different... genuine and without reservation. This time it was Mason that stood and watched me walk towards the door. Just before heading out into the parking lot, I turned around towards him and said, "It's pink and I have one older brother, his name is Matt."

He threw his head back in laughter as I disappeared into the sunlight.

CHAPTER NINE
February Seven ~ The Avett Brothers
Stomach Tied In Knots ~ Sleeping With Sirens

MASON

When Scarlett left the center that day, I felt better than I had in months. I knew that whatever she and I had shared in a romantic, couple-sense was over, but I still felt this overall sensation of calm and peace. I wasn't naïve enough to believe that just because she and I had talked, that all of my problems were going to be solved, but I knew it was a huge move in the right direction for both of us.

I went back to my room and grabbed my journal and guitar once again, and let the song that was screaming inside my head out. Up until that point, Scarlett had been the muse for many of the songs that I had written, but most of them were dark and depressing, lyrics about lost love and broken hearts. I had written enough tear-inducing ballads in my time at rehab to fill up two albums. Suddenly, I had a song begging to be written that celebrated the time we had shared together, and I began to furiously jot it down. After the last line, I set my pen down and knew that I had just written my first single for when I resumed my music career. It was perfect. Just perfect.

I had a little more than three weeks left in the center than another six at home for outpatient treatment. Heather had already begun talking to me about joining a support group once I was out. I was still a little hesitant about the idea, I wasn't a huge fan of the group sessions at the clinic as it was, but I wasn't completely ruling it out either. I also knew it would be hard to be a consistent attendee of a group once I went back on the road with Jobu's Rum.

I could not wait to get back to making music with my friends. It was my driving force now. I had been a part of the band for so long, I had forgotten what it was like to not be... and I hated it. I often found myself wondering what the guys were doing, especially Sebastian. I knew that he needed help just like I did. I only hoped that what had happened to me was somewhat of an eye opener for him. I had been scared to ask Cruz about it, but the more I thought about it, the more it began to eat at me. I picked up my phone and typed out a text.

> **ME: Hey man just thought I'd check in on you and the boys.**

CRUZ: Doing good. Hows you Rat boy?

ME: Better every day. I'm writing more music than Jobu's Rum will know what to do with

CRUZ: Awesome. Can't wait til ur home

ME: Hows Bastian doin? Plz tell me hes getting some help.

CRUZ: Yeah he got real freaked out after Miami. Hes not in a place or anything but hes seeing someone and he's been clean as far as I know.

ME: That's what I wanted to hear. Tell everyone I said what's up. I'll see y'all in a couple of months.

CRUZ: Will do. Can't wait.

An overwhelming feeling of relief came over me after reading Cruz' texts about Sebastian; everything seemed to be falling into place for me. I had made things right with Scarlett, my friends were getting their shit together and ready for me to return, and the drive to make music was stronger than it had ever been. I was actually starting to believe that I deserved to have things work out for me. Maybe I could learn to love myself after all.

SCARLETT

After I left the center, I couldn't stop thinking about the things that Heather had said in the session Mason and I had with her, especially the part about learning to love myself. If you had asked me prior to that conversation if I loved myself, my answer would have been "sure I do," but once I really started thinking about it, I began to question it. Did I love myself? Did I respect myself? Did I truly appreciate the person that I was?

Sighing aloud as those thoughts continued to assault my mind while I sat bored at work, I decided that I was in desperate need of a Chocolate Bar rendezvous with Max. Since we lived together now and talked to each other regularly at the apartment about what was going on in our lives, we had ditched our weekly dates at the dessert shop, but I was in desperate need of some chocolate, a latte, and some good advice. I texted him a message asking if he wanted to meet up there after I got off. He responded quickly, like he always did, that he would see me there.

As soon as I locked up the music store, I headed straight there, anxious to talk to Max about my visits with Mase. Walking through the glass doors, I grinned as I saw him waiting at our old table. Hurriedly, I walked over to him and threw my arms around his neck.

"Well, I'm glad to see you too, *sweetheart*," he said with the emphasis on the nickname.

I jokingly gave him a mean face as I sat across the table from him. "Hey *assface*, so glad you could make it."

"Assface? Really Scarlett, are you twelve?" He started laughing hard at my comment which in turn made me get the giggles."

"I have no idea where that came from, but I'm kinda liking it," I teased. "It suits you."

"No it doesn't," he protested, rubbing his hand over his face. "My face is quite gorgeous, if you haven't noticed."

"Nope, haven't noticed," I replied, rolling my eyes.

We continued to pick at each other back and forth for several minutes until he finally got serious and asked, "Okay Scarlett, really, why did you text me here? Something's gotta be up. Talk to me."

I drew quiet and looked down at my half-eaten chocolate covered twinkie, contemplating just how I went about saying what I needed to say.

Not coming up with any way to ease in the conversation, I looked up at him and blurted out, "I've been seeing Mase."

His back straightened, his eyes got big and he pounded his fist on the table, startling me. "Damn it, what in the world is wrong with you? Why would you cheat on Ash, Scarlett?"

"It... it's not what you think, Max," I stuttered. "I didn't mean like *seeing him*... I've been visiting him in rehab."

He relaxed a little in his chair, but I could tell he still wasn't pleased. "I'm guessing you haven't told Ash." I shook my head no. "And I'm guessing that's what you need help with..."

"I don't know what to say to him to make him understand that we really are just friends, and that things aren't like they used to be between us."

Max shook his head and rested his forehead against his palm. "Well my first word of advice is to not start out the convo with 'I've been seeing Mase.'"

I couldn't help but laugh at how horrible it sounded when he said it. "Yeah, that's probably not a good idea."

"Honestly, Scarlett, I'm not really sure what advice to give you. I can tell you that he's not gonna like it one bit. He thinks that even if you're intentions are pure and innocent, that Mason's aren't... and I can't really blame him."

"But we went to therapy together and talked about everything. We got it all out... the past, the things we did wrong... what we want from the future... all of it," I explained.

He raised his eyebrows and shook his head at me. "You've been going to therapy with him? Scarlett, how often have you been to see him?"

"Three times," I answered. "And today was the first time I had gone to the session with him. But I'm not gonna stop seeing him, Max. He needs a friend and I promised that I would be that for him."

"I know you mean well, but you have to think about Ash and how all of this will make him feel. I'm sure if the roles were reversed you wouldn't be gung ho about him being the friendly support for one of his ex-bimbos." He leaned forward and grabbed my hands again. "Look, I understand that you feel you have to save him, that you feel like this is at least partially your fault, but don't ruin things with Ash over this. I'm telling you that as a friend. Talk to Ash, see what he says... shit, maybe he's secure enough in y'all's relationship that he'll be okay with it. Just be prepared for an unpleasant reaction, okay sweetheart?"

I shook my head yes. I knew what he said was true, he wasn't trying to sugar coat any of it. I also knew that I wasn't going to let Mason down; I had to figure out a way to make everyone happy. "Thanks, Max. I'll tell him when I see him this weekend." We left the café together and went back to the apartment, never discussing the situation again.

~   ~   ~   ~   ~

Two days later, I went to visit Mase again and was pleased to find that the same progressive energy that I had felt when I left on Tuesday afternoon was still flowing freely between us. He was prepared for my arrival this time, it appeared he even styled his now shaggy hair and (gasp) put on socks. I teased him about it and got a kick out of the blush that covered his face.

We spent the afternoon with him trying to teach me how to play Xbox... again. For some reason, I just did not have the hand-eye coordination necessary to play video games. It was way too many buttons and things to pay attention to on the screen. Mase just laughed at my frustration.

"If you can play both the guitar and the piano, figuring out a control stick should be a piece of cake for you," he said as he ruffled my hair.

I turned around and gave him my mean face as the game to an end. I had two kills and suffered fourteen deaths. That was worse than terrible. "It's completely different," I argued. "When playing an instrument, you know what comes next in the song... it's static; when playing this stupid game, you have to react to what's going on around you. You can't pre-plan your actions."

"I promise you can figure this out, my studious little owl. You just need to practice," he encouraged me with a smile and a shoulder nudge.

Reminding myself that ten year old kids could play this game, I turned my attention back to the screen and controller and spent the following three hours practicing. Remarkably, at some point while I was playing, it was like a switch went off in my head and I all of a sudden, I was actually pretty decent. Mason got excited for me when he realized that the first two games that I ended up with more kills then deaths wasn't just a fluke.

"See!" he exclaimed. "I told you that you were smarter than the game."

Feeling smug with newfound skillset, even if it was mediocre at best, I began running my mouth. "Careful Mase, before you know it, I'll be kicking your ass as well as Ash and Max's."

As soon as Ash and Max's names crossed my lips, I instantly regretted it. The last thing I wanted to do was to throw either of them in Mason's face.

I guessed my face showed my remorse because he put his hand on my shoulder and immediately addressed my comment, "Angel, look at me." I raised my eyes to his, cringing a bit. "You don't need to feel bad about mentioning either of them. I understand that they are a part of your life, and that if you're gonna be in mine, so will they. I'm not sure how they feel about me..." He gave me one of his deep-dimpled grins. "Well, I have a pretty good idea, but I'm not gonna let that deter my friendship with you, as long as that's what you want."

I smiled meekly in return. "I've told Max that I've been coming to see you, but not Ash yet. I'm gonna tell him this weekend. I'm really scared that he's gonna freak."

He pulled me into a tight hug. "I'm not saying this just because we're talking about our friendship, but stop letting others make decisions for you. Do what you want to do. Live for Scarlett, no one else. It's what I'm trying to do too."

Our bodies broke apart and I couldn't help but feel a warmth inside me. "I'm not sure if I've told you yet, but I'm really proud of you, Mason. I'm proud to be your friend."

He kissed my forehead and whispered against my skin, "That's one step closer to my euphoria."

CHAPTER TEN

Where Did You Sleep Last Night ~ Nirvana
By Your Side ~ Tenth Avenue North

ASH

On that Thursday afternoon, I went home to grab a bite to eat in between my classes and working in the lab. I was sitting at the table, quietly enjoying my favorite cold weather combo, a grilled cheese sandwich and tomato soup, when I heard the postman on the front porch delivering the daily mail. I jumped up and ran outside to grab the stack of bills and letters. I had been anxiously awaiting the responses from the universities and research groups that I had applied to; I desperately wanted to know where I would be spending the next phase of my life so that I could begin making arrangements. Scarlett was my biggest concern. I refused to leave her, so wherever it was, I needed to convince her to transfer there with me. I knew that asking her to leave Rice, especially after the hurdles she had already faced was a huge request, but I wasn't going anywhere without her. Unfortunately, I had gone as far as I could possibly go at my current school with my degree in astrophysics, so staying in Houston wasn't an option.

As I thumbed through the envelopes, I set aside those items that were for Jess and those for Meg until I reached the envelope from the University of California Berkeley. My hands began shaking slightly as I opened the top of it, anxious to see the contents. UC Berkley was my number one choice by far because it had a research cooperative with the Lawrence Berkeley National Laboratory and a direct link to the CERN facility in Geneva, which was the mecca for nuclear physics. Despite my partying and womanizing in the college years before Scarlett, I had always put a major emphasis on my studies. I was blessed that a lot of it just came naturally to me; for whatever reason, I just "got" math and science. I had known from my high school years that I wanted to do something in the world of physics. Proving and disproving molecular theories was fascinating to me, and my ultimate goal had always been to work at CERN.

As I unfolded the single piece of paper, I held my breath and began to quickly scan over the text of the letter. It wasn't until I reached the words "We are pleased to inform you that we have accepted your application..." that I actually remembered to breathe again. I'm pretty sure if my neighbors had been home, they would've heard my roar of excitement. All of my hard work seemed to have started paying off; everything was falling into place. I just had to tell Scarlett.

The rest of the afternoon I could barely contain my enthusiasm, I was about to burst at the seams. I had told my boss the good news as soon as I had gotten to the lab, and he was not only extremely proud of me but understanding of my inability to focus. He let me off early to celebrate, so I went straight to Scarlett and Max's apartment to tell them my good news.

I was a little surprised to not see her car in her parking spot when I arrived, but didn't think too much of it. After several knocks, Max swung open the door and invited me in.

"Hey man, how are you? Come on in," he said as he walked over to sit back down on the couch.

"I couldn't be better actually, thanks for asking," I replied, still beaming. "Where's Scar?"

"Not sure. I haven't seen her since I've been home," he replied with a nonchalant shrug.

I found it odd that she wasn't home yet, seeing that it was nearly six o'clock in the evening. The night before she had told me that she had class until one and then she would be studying the rest of the afternoon. I assumed that she must've done her studying at the library or coffee shop, but since it was nearly dark outside I figured she'd be back soon. I grabbed a beer from the fridge and joined Max on the couch, waiting for her to get home.

Thirty minutes or so later, I was starting to get a little worried about where she was. I texted her and didn't get a reply, so I really began to panic. I got up to go throw my empty bottle away before heading over to the library to check for her car; however, when I was in the kitchen, I heard the front door open and then her voice.

"Hey Max! I'm so glad you're here! Mase taught me how to play Call of Duty today, and I can't wait to kick your pretty little assface."

My heart shattered all over the tile floor, and the overwhelming excitement that I had felt about my acceptance letter was replaced by complete devastation.

SCARLETT

As I hurried into the apartment, trying to escape the near freezing temperature outside, I was thrilled to see Max home so I could show off my new and improved Xbox playing abilities. However after my announcement of just that, Max's horror-stricken face followed by the sound of someone in the kitchen told me all that I needed to know. I could feel the color draining from my face as Ash appeared from around the corner. I couldn't tell if his expression was more of hurt or anger, but either way I didn't blame him. It definitely wasn't how I wanted him to find out, but since he knew I knew I better start talking fast before I lost him.

"Ash, babe, it's not what it seems. I promise," I tried to clarify, dropping my backpack and walking towards him.

"Oh, now it's 'babe,' huh? Convenient," he said with a snarl, backing away.

"I... I didn't mean..."

"And it never is what it seems when it involves him, is it Scarlett? In Miami it wasn't what it seemed, now here yet again, I get the same bullshit line." I had never heard such loathing in his voice before. "At some point Scarlett, it really IS what it seems!"

Thankfully, Max silently slipped out of the room in the middle of Ash's rant. Not that he wasn't able to hear it all from there anyhow, but at least we had perceived privacy.

"Ash, I know that you're angry, and I understand why. I had planned on telling you when I saw you this weekend. I didn't want to talk about it over the phone. I knew that you weren't going to be happy and I want to explain to you why. Please calm down. Let's sit down so that I can explain everything to you."

He stormed over to the couch and sat down. Looking up at me, he snapped, "I'm sitting so start explaining."

I crossed the living room floor and sat next to him. Wringing my hands in my lap with my eyes fixed on my shoes, I told him everything~ from Mina calling Cruz to my first visit to see Mase to our counseling session with Heather to that afternoon of just hanging out. I emphasized how we both felt closure with how our relationship previously had been, and we were only interested in being friends. After I was finished laying it all out, I looked up in his icy blue eyes and pled to him, "Ash, I swear on Evie's grave that I am telling you the truth. I know that I should've told you when I first went, but I am hiding nothing from you and am being one hundred percent honest with you about my feelings for him. I am in love with *you* and I want to be with *you*, but I am going to be a friend to him. He is far from perfect, just like both of us, but he has always been there for me when I needed him and I'm not about to turn my back on him, especially during this time of instability. I really hope you can understand that."

"I do understand that Scarlett, but you have to know how hard this is for me. I know what he once was to you, and it scares me that those feelings between y'all will reemerge. I don't associate with any girls that I have a past with, and I never even had true feeling for any of them. I do that mainly because I have no desire to be around those people any longer, I've grown up and moved on from that stage of my life, but also because I have respect for your feelings. I know that you wouldn't feel comfortable with me even being just friends with them.

"I honestly feel like I'm painted in a corner here. Either I give you my blessing to see him or I risk losing you if I don't. You know I'm not the type of person to tell you what you can or can't do; we don't have that kind of relationship. So I'm going to tell you this one time and one time only." He paused and took a deep breath before continuing. "You are an adult and you need to decide who you have relationships with. That being said, I expect for you to put me first in your life, just like I do with you in mine. I don't need daily or even weekly updates on what's going on with him, because I really don't care, but I don't want this cutting into the time we get to spend together either. I love you and I'm going to trust you until you give me a reason not to, but I will not be made a fool of. I deserve to get back the same commitment that I put into this. Do you think that's fair?"

I nodded my head before launching myself at him. I crawled into his lap, my knees on either sides of his thighs, and pressed my forehead to his. "Thank you so much. Thank you for being so wonderful. You are always my first priority and I'm not gonna let you down. I love you so much."

His strong arms engulfed my waist and he pulled my chest down to his. His soft lips found mine, tenderly pressing them against each other before his tongue began teasing me, begging entrance into my mouth. Parting my lips, our tongues found one another, delicately caressing and massaging into the perfect kiss. As the kiss ended and our mouths broke apart, a thought crossed my mind.

"Not that I ever mind seeing you or kissing you, but was there a reason that you came over tonight or was it just to hang out?" I asked him before giving him another soft peck on the mouth.

He stood up with me still wrapped around his body and rubbed his nose against mine. "Nah, it wasn't anything important really. Plus I don't want to spend any more time talking tonight; I need to feel your body against mine. I think it's time for another reminder fuck," he growled.

My body responded to the possessive tone in his voice, as I instantly ached for his intimate touch. I clenched my legs tightly around his body so that my clit rubbed against his crotch and I nipped at his bottom lip before sucking on it. "What are you reminding me of?"

"That. You. Are. Mine." He walked us down the hall to my bedroom where he spent the next couple of hours reminding me of just that.

CHAPTER ELEVEN
Nothing Fancy ~ Dave Barnes
Burn ~ Ellie Goulding
Together ~ Demi Lovato (feat. Jason Derulo)

ASH

I knew that I should've told her about the doctorate program acceptance letter when she asked why I had come over, but I just couldn't. Not then. We needed to deal with one issue at a time, and in that moment, pretty much everything else was on the backburner. I also decided to wait to confirm that she had gotten accepted at UC Berkeley as well so that I could present it to her as a package deal. I had to make her see the future for us there... away from here.

To be honest, as Scarlett told me the story about how she had gone to see Mason in rehab, I believed her that she truly was worried about him as a person and that her intentions were to be his friend and to help him through his recovery. It was him that I didn't trust for shit, especially in a time where he was sure to feel abandoned by his friends, his fans, and his steady stream of groupies falling at his feet. He was an attention whore, plain and simple. I had never met a frontman of a band that wasn't, that's why they were what they were. My musical skills were just as good, if not better than his, but I never had any desire to be up in front of hundreds or thousands of people. He craved the spotlight and it fed his egotism and vanity, and having her coming to visit him, to coddle him, was just another form of that. However, I also knew if I forbade her from seeing him, she would either resent me or see him anyway behind my back. Either of those scenarios would end in us breaking up, which was the last thing I wanted.

After worshipping her body for most of the night, reminding her exactly who it was that gave her everything she needed, we both skipped our early morning class and slept in, staying warm and cozy under the covers. I really wanted to do something special and fun with her that weekend. It seemed like ever since we had officially been together as a couple, it was always something causing a strain on our relationship. When we had come back from California, first it was Mina and Noah's wedding, then it was Mason's overdose, and for the past couple of weeks it had been the stress of classes in the new semester. We had never really had any time for ourselves, so I wanted to get her away for a couple of days.

I slipped out of bed while she was still in dreamland and made a few calls to set everything up. When she finally decided to roll out of bed a little after eleven, I told her to get showered up and to pack a bag because we were going away for a surprise weekend getaway. The smile that lit up her face when I told her warmed my soul, and I couldn't wait to get us away from there. I ran home, got ready myself, and packed up some clothes. A little more than an hour later, I had Scarlett secured in my front seat and we were heading west on I-10.

"Are you gonna tell me where we are going?" she asked, obviously both excited and curious as we pulled out of her apartment complex.

"Nope," I teased her. "You'll know when we get there."

"Well, how long of a drive is it?"

"Just a couple of hours. Settle down Nervous Nellie, it will be fun, I promise.

She gave me that signature Scarlett smile and melted my heart. "Ok, I trust you. I just like being prepared for where I'm going and who I'm going to be around."

I grabbed her hand and brought it to my mouth, kissing the top of her knuckles. "Other than the hotel staff, I'm the only person you need to worry about being around."

True to my word, about three hours later we pulled up to Lake Austin Spa Resort. After a quick check in with the front desk, I retrieved the keys to our premier hot tub cabin and I drove the car around to our home for the next two nights. When we entered cabin, she was like a little kid on Christmas morning, looking around at everything, taking it all in. She was beaming from ear to ear, and I knew that I had made the right decision. When she made her way to the French doors in the back of the cabin, she opened them and found the back porch decked out with a hot tub and posh sitting area that had breathtaking views of the lake.

"It's absolutely gorgeous, Ash," she whispered in her sweet little voice. She turned around and launched herself into my arms. "Thank you so much for bringing me here. It's perfect."

I enveloped her tightly in my arms, burying my face in her hair, savoring her heavenly smell. "You're welcome, butterfly; anything for you."

Sunday afternoon came before either of us wanted it to. We had spent forty eight hours being completely pampered at the spa and divulging into the delicious meals prepared by the chefs. My mom and sister had always gone to get massages and pedicures when I was growing up, and I had never quite understood the draw to it, but after that weekend, I had a newfound respect for the relaxation and rejuvenation those things did for one's well-being. Spending that time alone away with Scarlett was therapeutic not only on an individual level, but for us as a couple as well. We spent hours upon hours in the hot tub under the stars talking about our hopes and dreams for the future. I told her all about CERN and my obsession with the research that was going on there. She expressed to me her love for music, which was much deeper than I had ever realized. She hadn't done much with it scholastically because she was afraid of what her parents and others would think of her wasting away a Rice education just to major in music theory. I encouraged her to follow her heart with it. She would only be miserable if she ended up working in the business world if her true calling was in music. I hoped that I had gotten through to her, even if it was just a little, and I was going to continue to push her to follow her dream. On several occasions I had the opportunity to tell her about California, but I didn't want to ruin the moment with a possible argument, plus I still didn't know for sure where she could enroll once we got there. I knew everything would work out. Like I had always told her, I had faith that fate would find a way.

SCARLETT

When Ash and I came back from our weekend at the lake, I was completely revitalized and felt as if I had a direction for my future. I had been struggling with the whole "what do you want to be when you grow up" topic for some time now. Other than my music, I really had nothing else that I felt connected to. All of my classes came pretty easy to me for the most part, but I didn't love any of them. Even though they had always pushed my music lessons on me, my parents had always made me feel like there was no future in it, that it wasn't an acceptable career choice. However after talking to Ash about it, I began to realize that there was nothing disgraceful at all in following your calling. Even if I was an elementary school music teacher forever, I would be doing something that I absolutely loved; it didn't matter how much money I did or didn't make nor what my parents thought about it.

After he dropped me off at my apartment that evening, I unpacked my things and changed into my pajamas. I had been hoping Max would be there so I could tell him all about the weekend, but he was nowhere to be found. I also couldn't wait to tell Mason about my decision. I thought about texting him, but decided I would wait to tell him in person on Tuesday when I went to see him. I knew he would be proud of me for going after something I really wanted. I was accepting who I was and what I wanted, and I was finally learning to embrace it. I felt as if things were finally starting to make sense for me.

All of the talk and thinking about music also made me realize that other than when I was bored at work, I hardly ever played anymore. It had been a long time since I had learned to play anything new as well. I pulled my keyboard out of my closet and pulled up the sheet music to Ellie Goulding's *Burn,* which I was totally in love with. For the next couple of hours I completely lost myself in the song; I allowed the music to take over, my fingers moving fluidly over the keys as I belted out the lyrics. Not even aware that Max had come home, he nearly scared the life out of me when his voice joined me mid chorus during my concert for one. I looked over my shoulder at him and smiled as he climbed onto my bed next to me, neither of us missing a note.

When we finished the song, he began clapping and whistling. "Bravo! Bravo! My dear Scarlett, when did you learn how to play the piano?"

"Umm, when I was about six," I teased as I nudged his shoulder with mine.

"I knew you played the guitar, but I had no idea about this... and your voice! Why don't you do anything with this talent? You're amazing sweetheart."

Slightly blushing, I told him my news. "Well, actually I decided over this weekend that I am going to do something with it. I've always felt like it was just something to do as a hobby, but after talking with Ash this weekend he helped me realize that if I really love it, which I do, that I should pursue it. So when I got home, I pulled this old thing out," I explained as I nodded to the keyboard.

"I'm really in shock. I just never realized," he said beaming down at me. Abruptly, he jumped off the bed. "Hold on, I'm gonna grab my guitar. I want to play with you."

A few minutes later, Max and I were holding quite the concert on my bed. We played anything and everything that we both knew how to play by memory; I'm sure our neighbors just loved us. I then thought of a song that was perfect for the two of us.

"How quickly can you pick up music from a tab sheet?" I asked him.

He rolled his eyes at me. "So do you not know who I am? I am the guitarist for the world-renowned Thirty Two Leaves," he retorted, acting annoyed.

"Oh well, excuse me," I said playfully. I put the iPad in his lap with *Together* pulled up on it. "In that case, here read over this while I play the song for you to listen to. I'll expect you to nail it on the first try."

After we listened to it a couple of times, he said, "Okay, I think I've got it. Let's give it a go." And nail it, he did. We sounded amazing, if I do say so myself. Even he knew it. "Okay let's try it again, but dirty it up a little. It's a little too bubblegum for both of our voices," he suggested.

I nodded excitedly, completely understanding what he was saying. Our voices harmonized perfectly together, and after just a couple of run throughs, we had pretty much perfected it.

Looking at the clock on my nightstand, I saw that it was after two in the morning. Max's eyes followed mine and he laughed. "Yes, we better both get some sleep. I'm afraid our song won't help us pass any of our classes this semester." He kissed me on the forehead before getting off the bed. "Get some sleep, rockstar. We'll play again tomorrow."

I slipped in between my cool sheets as he walked out of my room. Just before he closed the door behind him, he stuck his head in and said, "If Noah and the rest of the guys are okay with it, would you ever be interested in doing a song or two with us up at Empty's?"

I lifted my head off of the pillow and looked at him in disbelief. "Are you serious?"

"Yes, I'm serious, silly. You're really incredible" he answered, smiling brightly.

"Absolutely. I'd love it."

"Okay, I'll let you know what they say. Goodnight, sweetheart."

"Goodnight Max."

CHAPTER TWELVE
Wake Me Up ~ Avicci
The Forgotten ~ Green Day

MASON

One more day. I had one more day in the rehab center before I rejoined the rest of society, and to be quite honest, I was a little nervous. Despite my initial denial that I even needed help to begin with, my mindset towards how I viewed both myself and others was completely different five weeks after walking through those doors. The clarity in which I was beginning to see things with was incredible, and learning how to make decisions in the best interest of me without being a selfish asshole was becoming attainable.

Scarlett's visits every Tuesday and Thursday afternoon were the bright spots of my week. I was thrilled when she told me about her decision to follow her musical dreams. Of course, as a musician myself, I knew the fulfillment that it helped bring to my life, and I really wanted her to find true happiness as well, wherever that was. It had become apparent that any hope of Scarlett and I ever being together in a romantic sense was all but nonexistent, no matter what I wanted, but I still wanted the absolute best life for her. Our relationship while I was in the center had blossomed into an amazing friendship. I had always known that she was sweet, compassionate, and had a heart of gold, but I discovered that she had an amazing sense of humor and was fun to just hang out with. My desire to touch her smooth porcelain skin or kiss her soft pink lips had not disappeared, but I learned to push it to the back of my mind. Her being in my life, in whatever capacity, made me a better person; I'd take my angel any way I could get her.

I had decided that I wanted to stay at my apartment in Houston for the six weeks post release for a couple of reasons. First, I could continue my therapy with Heather if I stayed in the city, and I had formed a great bond with her. Sometimes it was hard to remember that she was my counselor and not my friend. I knew at some point I would be leaving both her and Houston to rejoin the band in Austin, but I thought another six weeks with her rather than starting over with a new therapist would be the best thing for me.

That night after dinner, several of the other patients that I had become friends with all stopped by my room to hang out for a while. Someone asked me what the first thing I was going to do when I got out was, and my reply was go to McDonalds. After everyone laughed a bit, they each began talking about what they couldn't wait to do. Answers ranged from seeing friends to apologizing to parents to having sex until it got to one girl, Andi, who said, "I never want to leave." The response stunned me, so I immediately asked why. "There's nothing out there for me. My family doesn't want me and I don't have many real friends, so there's really no where for me to go that's not going to lead me right back here again," she said matter-of-factly with a shrug.

My heart broke for her. I couldn't imagine feeling hopelessness like that. I didn't have much family either, Marcus was it for me. Even though he and I didn't always see eye to eye, I couldn't imagine having no one at all. As for friends, I was blessed in that department. Cruz had been my best friend since we were little kids, I knew he had my back no matter what. Slowly throughout school we had added his cousin Sebastian and then Aaron to our group, and even as much as I whined about Aaron's girlfriend, Sophie, she had always been a good friend to me. Then there was Scarlett. I knew I could depend on her no matter what. The fact we had salvaged a friendship after everything we had been through was proof that we weren't going anywhere in each other's lives.

Bringing my attention back to the group, conversation had moved to what everyone's favorite restaurant was. The small group hung out until it was time for lights out and then I said my final goodbyes and wished them all the best.

Before Andi walked out the door, I asked her to stay back a minute. I had never really paid much attention to her; she was tiny in stature and typically very quiet during group activities and just kind of stayed to herself. She always hid behind her long dark hair and baggy clothes. As she looked up at me, the surprise evident in her big blue eyes, I asked her, "When do you get out?"

"Whenever I want really. I've been here for nearly five months now. My parents just keep paying because they don't want to deal with me. Their life is easier if I'm here."

I visibly frowned, not even trying to hide my displeasure. "How old are you?"

"I turned eighteen last week." Damn she was just a baby. I didn't understand why parents would rather keep their kid locked up in here rather than at home where they could actually be parents.

"What are you in here for?"

"What am I not in here for?" She laughed nervously as she pushed her hands into her pockets.

"Don't answer my question with a question please. I want to know what your drug of choice is," I said sternly.

"I've dabbled in pretty much everything but my addiction is not alcohol or drug related. Blood is my drug of choice," she replied as her eyes pierced mine. "I cut."

"Oh," was the only thing I managed to say. Her answer caught me completely off guard and it took me a minute to wrap my head around it. She stood there staring at me, with a snarky look on her face, "Any other questions *Dad?*"

"You don't need to get defensive with me," I said calmly. "I was going to tell you if wanted a place to stay on the outside, that I have a two bedroom apartment that you are more than welcome to stay at. My brother owns a bar and I could get you a job, but if alcohol was your issue, that probably wouldn't be the best idea. I wasn't trying to be your dad, I was trying to be your friend."

Her face relaxed as she realized what I was offering to her. "Why would you do that for me? You don't know me; how can you trust me?"

"You're right, I don't. However, if you really don't have anyone or anywhere to go, I would hope you're a decent enough person, that you wouldn't screw over the one person trying to help you. Unless you really do want to live here forever..."

Before I knew it, she flew across the room and was sobbing in my arms. "You are the nicest person I have ever met. I can't believe you just said all of that. Are you some kind of guardian angel or something?"

Laughing, I answered, "No, not even close, but I am taking notes from one. You'll meet her tomorrow." She pulled back and cocked her head at me confused. I continued, "If you accept the offer, one of my closest friends, Scarlett, who truly is an angel, will be picking me up to take me home tomorrow. Since you're eighteen and have finished the program, I'm guessing you can check yourself out at any time? So I thought she could take us both at the same time.

She began jumping up and down in my arms, grinning from ear to ear. She really was a cute girl once you found her face behind all of that hair. "Yes! Yes! I will pack up my stuff tonight and discharge myself in the morning."

"There are rules in the apartment, Andi. Absolutely no drugs whatsoever, not even pot. I can't be around any of it. If you do decide to work at the bar, alcohol can't become an issue; you will lose your job. Don't steal from me; please don't fucking steal from me. And you've got to continue counseling for the cutting. If I find out you're doing it again, I will drive your ass back here in a heartbeat." I looked at her sternly. "Are you cool with all of that?"

"Yes, absolutely."

"Also, in six weeks, I will be commuting back and forth between Houston and Austin, so I won't be there all of the time. Not that it should be an issue, but just so you know," I warned her.

"Oh my God, I can't believe this. I promise I won't disappoint you," she said as she left my room, obviously ecstatic.

"I sure hope not," I mumbled to myself. Shaking my head, I stripped off my shirt and jeans and climbed into my bed wondering what in the fuck I had just done. I had invited a strange girl that had admitted issues with cutting herself to live with me. Maybe I was taking the selfless thing a bit too far... Oh well, it was too late at that point. It truly did make me feel incredible inside to do something for her. She desperately needed someone to believe in her, like Scarlett had done with me; I just hoped it wouldn't backfire on me.

SCARLETT

Waking up the morning I was to pick Mase up from rehab, I was excited and anxious. Proud didn't even begin to describe how I felt about the progress he had made while there. It wasn't that he was a different person than I once knew, he was just a new and very much improved version of it. He still had confidence but without the over-the-top cockiness and his egotism had been replaced with pure charm and charisma. Physically, I kind of liked the longer locks and scruffy facial hair, but he had already told me that he couldn't wait to shave his head and face as soon as he got out.

I pulled up promptly at ten o'clock in the morning, just as I had promised him. Ash was none too happy that I was spending a Saturday morning doing something with Mase since he deemed that as his time, but I didn't give him an option. I was picking him up to take him home and that was it. End of.

I hurried through the front glass doors, signing in at the front desk before heading to Mason's room. Needless to say, I was more than surprised to find someone else in Mason's room when I poked my head in. He and a dark-haired girl were sitting on his bed laughing about something when I entered and asked, "Are you all ready to go?"

Both of them looked up at the sound of my voice and smiled at me. He stood up and walked over to where I stood, right inside the door frame and hugged me tightly. "Morning, angel," he said in his husky voice. "I'm so glad you're here; I've never been more ready for anything." As he backed away, he looked over at the girl on the bed and then back at me. "Scarlett, I would like you to meet Andi. Andi, this is my angel I was telling you about."

Not wanting to be rude, even though a hundred questions shot through my mind about who this person was and why she was in his room, I walked over to her and extended my hand with a smile. "Nice to meet you, Andi."

She shook my hand and smiled meekly. "Thank you so much for coming to get us," she said in a voice barely above a whisper .

Coming to get *them*? Instantly my head spun around to look at him questioning what in the world she was talking about, and why in the world had he never mentioned this Andi girl before? I had been there twice a week for over a month and never once had he said her name. I felt like I was really missing something.

Mason bit his bottom lip nervously and gave me a look that I couldn't quite read. "Scarlett, Andi is going to stay in the other bedroom at the apartment and work at Empty's until she can enroll in school next fall. She's coming with us today."

A multitude of emotions flooded me at his announcement, jealousy more than anything. I knew that I had no right to feel that way, I had a boyfriend and a male roommate, so why couldn't he have one or both? I took a brief second to push aside my selfish and unfair thoughts, and then turned back to the girl. "That's wonderful, Andi. I'm sure that you'll love working at the bar, it's a fun atmosphere, and that's great to hear that you want to get back in school. If there's any way that I can help you please let me know."

Still smiling at me with her bright blue eyes, she said timidly, "That is so sweet of you. He told me that you were the nicest person that I'd ever meet, and I can see why." Her kind words made me feel like a bitch for the thoughts that had crossed my mind. I really needed to get over myself and be a friend to this poor girl. Obviously Mason had a reason for helping her out and I needed to live up to the person that he, and now she, thought that I was. Less than thirty minutes later, their bags were in my trunk, and we were pulling out of the parking lot heading to the closest McDonalds and then off to their apartment.

CHAPTER THIRTEEN
The Story of My Life ~ Kristian Leontiou
Bittersweet ~ Ellie Goulding

ASH

Mason getting out of rehab worried the shit out of me. It wasn't like I expected him to stay there forever, but his release seemed to happen way too quickly. Even though I wasn't a huge fan of Scarlett spending time with him, at least when he was in the center, I felt like their visits were somewhat supervised. With him being back in his apartment, I really didn't want her hanging out over there, but what could I really say at that point. I had agreed to trust her, so trust her I did.

The day she went to pick him up I was a mess, a ball of nervous energy. It was a Saturday, which was a day I usually spent in its entirety with her, so I wasn't thrilled about giving up one of *my* days. Of course I woke up earlier than usual that morning, and after lying there looking at my ceiling for almost an hour, I decided to grab my long board and head to the local skate park for an early morning ride. That did help me keep my mind off of things for the couple of hours that I was there, but as soon as I was back at my house, I began wondering what they were doing. Both Jess and Meg were still asleep so I didn't want to play the guitar; they probably wouldn't appreciate being woken up on a weekend morning. I tried sketching for a little while, but I was just getting frustrated with that too.

I decided to go visit my mom for a bit; she always made me feel better. I stopped and got an assortment of breakfast pastries and fresh fruit before making my way to her condo. As I waited at her door after knocking several times, I thought maybe I should've called before showing up unannounced. Finally, she opened the door and greeted me, "Ash, son, it's so good to see you. What brings you by this morning?" I could tell there was something off in her voice immediately.

I leaned down to kiss her on the cheek and said, "I just thought I'd bring by some breakfast and visit for a bit. I haven't seen you in a few weeks."

She kept her body in the doorframe, not moving to let me in, and looked down at the bag of food in my hands. That's when I heard the deep male voice from inside her place. "Robin, is everything okay? Who was at the door?"

I'm not sure who's eyes grew larger as we stood there, silently staring at each other. Then the voice spoke again. "Robin? What are you doing? Get back in bed."

I shook my head and swallowed down the sick feeling that crept up my throat. "I'm sorry I came at a bad time. You should probably get back in bed," I croaked. I didn't wait for her to say anything, I turned on my heel and took off down the hallway. I heard her call after me, but I didn't bother looking back. The day was only getting worse.

I had no patience to wait for the elevator, so I bound down the stairs, taking two and three at a time, anxious to get outside into the fresh air. I threw open the door and nearly tumbled outside. Hurrying to get inside the safety of my car, I plopped myself into the driver's seat and sat there wondering what to do next.

With no destination in mind, I started the engine and pulled out of the parking area and just drove. I could feel the tears threatening, but I was determined to not cry. I was being ridiculous and crying wasn't going to make anything better. Twenty minutes later I found myself at the zoo. Why in the fuck was I at the zoo? I didn't question it, I just got out and made my way towards the entrance. I gave some homeless people that were loitering on the park benches the bag of food and just kept walking until I was inside the gates.

For most of the afternoon, I spent walking around looking at the exhibits. It had been a really long time since I had been there, actually the last time I could remember was my mom bringing me and Crys for one of my birthdays, when I was like eight or nine. I looked around at the other families that were there and I was a bit envious of the time they were spending together. I realized just how much I missed those times with my mom and my sister. I sat down at one of the benches around the reflection pond and dialed Crys' number.

"If it isn't my favorite brother," she answered the phone cheerfully, not even bothering to say hello.

Her voice alone put a smile on my face. "I'm your only brother, Crys. It's not much of a competition."

"When did you become such a pessimist? And why are you calling me so damn early?" She asked teasing.

"It's after eleven o'clock here, and I figured with your rugrats you would be awake already."

I could hear her sigh. "Yes, these nephews of yours don't know what the words 'sleeping in' mean." As if on cue, I heard a crashing noise in the background followed by yelling of whose fault it was. "See, just another day of paradise going on here."

"Do I need to call back at a better time?"

Chuckling, she retorted, "Sure, how does fourteen years from now work for you? I think I may be able to get through a phone call uninterrupted about that time."

"No, that won't work for me at all," I said, playing along. "I have dinner plans that night."

"Well then, I suppose you'll have to tell me the reason for this phone call now. I'm sure you didn't just decide to call up your old sister out of the blue to check on me. What's going on? Everything okay with you and Scarlett?"

Groaning, I began telling her about my shitty day. "Actually, I'm just having an awful day... one of those where everything is going wrong, ya know? For some reason I'm at the zoo right now."

"Why in the world are you at the zoo?" she screeched in my ear.

"I don't know honestly. I just kind of ended up here. I was walking around and I started thinking about the last time I was here and I remembered that time mom brought you and me for my birthday."

"Awww my baby brother's taking a stroll down memory lane; shit must be really fucked up. What in the world happened?"

Not beating around the bush any longer, "I took mom breakfast this morning and there was a guy there. She wouldn't even let me inside."

"Okay..."

"Did you not here me, Crys? I said there was a man there... like he called her back to bed; it was horrific. I thought I was going to be sick right there."

"Ash, Mom is a fifty five year old single woman. She's allowed to have someone stay over. Do you honestly expect her to be celibate the rest of her life now that she's divorced?" Her laughter at me just infuriated me more.

"No, I don't! Well, maybe... I don't know! I don't want to think about it. It's gross," I retorted angrily.

"I totally just rolled my eyes at you. You're being ridiculous," she scolded me. "Did you call her before you showed up at her front door? I'm assuming probably not."

"Well, no. But..."

"Do you want her showing up at your house unannounced early in the morning?"

"Well, no."

"Okay, then. Calm down, she's an adult. Stop being so selfish, you should want her to be happy. Now what's really going on because there had to be a reason you took Mom breakfast if it wasn't a planned visit?" I could hear her shuffling about and whispering something. "Okay, I just sent Will outside with the boys and I'm pouring a new cup of coffee. Start talking."

I spent the next half hour sitting on a bench in the park telling my sister everything from Scarlett and Mason's friendship and her helping him out with his recovery to the acceptance letter to UC Berkeley to filling out applications for Scarlett without her knowing. The following half hour was spent listening to her scold me about my selfish behavior and her telling me in every possible way that I was acting like an ass about the Mom and Scarlett situations. By the time we ended the call, Crys had successfully brought me back to reality and I knew what I needed to do to make things right.

As I drove back to my house that afternoon, I called my mom and apologized to her for both showing up at her house without calling and for my childish reaction once I found that she wasn't alone. I told her that I did want her to be happy and promised to be more understanding. Hearing the joy in her voice after I said what I needed to, elated me immensely. We exchanged "I love you's," and said goodbye as I pulled into my driveway. I grabbed the mail from the box just before going into the house and tossed it on the kitchen table as I headed back to my room. I quickly typed out a text to Scarlett before stripping out of my clothes and jumping in the shower.

> **Me: Hey butterfly, I hope everything went good today. If you are free tonight, I'd love to see ya. I'm about to take a shower but after that I'll just be chillin at the house.**

SCARLETT

I was turning on to Ash's street when his text came through on my phone. I looked down at my phone, smiling, I had missed not hearing from him all day. I didn't know if he was upset with me since I had spent a Saturday with Mason or if he was busy doing things on his own.

My day had not gone quite as planned, beginning with picking up not just Mase, but Andi too from the center. Once we got to the apartment, I realized that I had underestimated the emotions that I would feel being back in the place that he and I once lived as a couple. I didn't even want to go back into his bedroom, I wasn't sure that I could see the bed that we had shared intimately. In addition, I couldn't figure out their relationship at all; it seemed as if they didn't know each other very well, which I couldn't decide if that made me happy or not. Either they were great actors or there really was nothing going on between them romantically. I could never get Mase alone to ask him who she was or what was going on with the whole situation. She seemed nice enough, a little on the quiet side, but very appreciative to both me and him. I took them both to Super Target so that they could stock up on groceries, toiletries, and other things that they needed. She had mentioned that she had never lived on her own before, and when she went to pay, she used an American Express platinum card. The entire scenario continued to get more and more bizarre as the day went on, but I just did what any good friend would, I smiled and stayed supportive.

Once we got all of the food put away in the refrigerator and pantry and the rest of the plastic bags unpacked, I decided to leave them to get some rest. They both seemed to be pretty exhausted. I couldn't imagine the emotional or mental mindset of either of them, having just been released from rehab. I wasn't sure what Andi's addiction problems were, but I hoped that Mase had really thought about that thoroughly. I didn't know the first thing about how the rehabilitation process worked, but two recovering addicts living together didn't seem like such a good idea to me... or maybe it was, maybe they could support each other and hold the other accountable... I really had no idea. I supposed it really didn't matter at that point, it was a done deal.

As I was leaving the apartment, both of them thanked me several times for my help and Mase gave me a tight hug with a kiss on the forehead before I made my way out the door. As soon as I got in my car, I decided I didn't want to spend the rest of my evening wondering what in the world had just happened, so I drove straight to Ash's house.

I skipped up the front walk and tapped my knuckles on the door, anxious to see him. After several knocks with no response, I assumed he was still in the shower and grabbed the spare key from under the flower pot, letting myself inside.

"Hello? Anyone home?" I called out as I walked through the front door. No one responded but I heard the shower running in the back of the house, confirming my previous assumption. Before heading back to Ash's room, I got a coke out of the refrigerator and as I walked by the kitchen table, an envelope with my name in the pile of mail caught my eye. Curious to why something addressed to me would be coming to his house, I opened the letter and read it. Completely confused and more than a little irritated, I went to his room and waited for him to get out of the shower.

Several minutes later, I heard the water turn off and shortly thereafter, he walked into his room, wearing only a towel around his waist. As soon as he saw me sitting on his bed, he smiled and said, "Wow! That was fast!"

When he leaned down to kiss me, I put the letter in front of my face to block his advance. "Do you want to explain what this is?"

CHAPTER FOURTEEN
Can't Stand Me Now ~ The Libertines
Over You ~ Miranda Lambert
All of Me ~ John Legend

ASH

When Scarlett shoved the letter in front of my face, my heart sunk into my stomach. I had planned on coming clean about everything that night, I really had, but this definitely wasn't the way I wanted her to find out. I was stunned silent for a moment as I briefly skimmed over the letter that she held up. Not knowing the best way to approach the subject now, I just decided to be brutally honest.

"It's an acceptance letter into UC Berkeley," I answered.

"Why is it addressed to me?" Both her hands and her voice were shaking as she asked the question.

I took the letter from her hands and sat down next to her on the bed, still in just my towel. "I know you probably aren't going to believe me, but I was going to tell you all about this and everything else tonight or the next time I saw you."

"Everything else? What in the fuck is going on, Ash? Why have I been accepted into some college that I didn't apply to?" The confusion was quickly turning into anger and I knew that I needed to start explaining fast.

"Let me put some clothes on so that we can talk," I said as I slid off the bed and walked over to my dresser. I swiftly threw on some boxers and pajama pants and then rejoined her on the bed. She just sat there staring at me, making no attempt to hide her displeasure; I was expecting either steam to start rising from her head or a flood of tears to fall from her big brown eyes at any minute.

"Okay, so here's the deal. As you know I'm finishing up my Master's degree this May, so I've been applying to several different universities to enter their doctorate programs. I knew that if I was accepted into any of these, I'd have to move and I wanted you to come with me wherever I went. So without talking to you first, I took it upon myself to apply for a transfer for you to each of these schools as well. I thought that once I found the right place where we could both go, I'd present it to you and you'd want to go together. I didn't want to tell you and stress you out until I knew that we were both in."

"So let me get this straight... you were basically deciding my future for me. You weren't giving me any say in what school I go to or where I live?"

"Well there are only a handful of schools that offer a PhD program in nuclear astrophysics, so I applied to all of them for both of us. I mean, of course you have the option to not come with me, but I thought that this...," I explained as I moved my hand back and forth between our two bodies, "I thought we were for forever, so I assumed that you would want to go."

"Do you hear yourself right now? Do you hear the words coming out of your mouth? You're no better than my parents who tried to control me forever. You're completely planning my future for me, without even discussing it with me!"

"That wasn't my intention, Scarlett..."

"No! It's my turn to talk," she interrupted me. "You of all people... the person that has been so adamant about me learning to make decisions on my own, to live my life for me, to not let others control me... you're such a hypocrite! That's exactly what you've done, or are trying to do. I can't believe this." She jumped off the bed and began pacing around my room.

"I'm so sorry. I didn't even think about it like that. I thought if when I told you about it, I had all the facts together, you wouldn't have to worry about anything. I promise you, butterfly, I didn't mean for it to seem like I was taking away your decision. If you would've said no to all of them, then we would've figured out something else." My voice was now shaking, but with fear instead of anger as hers was.

"We would've figured something else out? Like you wouldn't have continued your education? Bull shit! And don't even with the 'butterfly' crap right now, that's a fucking joke. You don't want me to grow wings and learn how to fly, you want me in a little cocoon where you can control me just like everyone else!"

"Scarlett, please calm down. I know you're mad; I know that I fucked this up, and I'm desperately trying to tell you that I'm sorry. I was going to tell you about everything, even without knowing that the letter came. I talked to Crys today and she made me realize that I was being a selfish asshole, especially with the way I handled this. I'm sorry! I want to know what you want. Please, let's talk about this," I pleaded with her.

"What I want right now is some time by myself. I need to cool off and time to think. I'll call you later." She picked up her purse and keys off of my bed and stomped out of the room. I desperately wanted to call after her, to chase after her and beg her not to leave, but I didn't. I let her walk out the door, hoping and praying that it wasn't for good... hoping and praying she wouldn't run to his arms again.

SCARLETT

Anger didn't even begin to cover the emotion that was coursing through my veins. Rage... fury... disappointment... irritation... outrage. I couldn't stop shaking as I escaped Ash's house and got into my car. I was so overwhelmed with everything that I had just found out, I couldn't even cry. It was almost as if I was feeling so much, that I just went numb, like a defense mechanism so that I didn't have a complete mental breakdown.

I needed someone to talk to badly. I couldn't talk to Mase about this; he didn't need any of my issues to stress about especially on his first day home with a new roommate. I could go home and talk to Max, but I felt like all I did was cry about my life to him. Plus, if I found out that he knew about what Ash had done, I was going to be livid with him as well. I tried calling Mina, but she didn't answer; she was probably out with Noah somewhere, as she usually was. I really needed my Evie in that moment. I missed her all the time, but I really fucking needed her right then.

I drove straight to the cemetery; it was where I had to go, the only place that I felt I could find some solace. I parked my car not far from her gravesite and grabbed my jacket out of the backseat. The sun was disappearing into the horizon and the frigid February night was setting in rapidly. It had only been a couple of months since I had been there at the one year anniversary of her death, but so much had happened in that short amount of time. I trudged my way over to her headstone and knelt down in front of it. The ground was frozen and the wetness of the soil quickly soaked through the knees of my jeans, but I barely noticed.

EVELYN ROSE STEWART
April 27, 1993 ~ December 10, 2012

And if you were with me tonight
I'd sing to you just one more time
A song for a heart so big
God wouldn't let it live
May angels lead you in.

As I read the words on her grave again, the tears finally came. And boy did they come. I sat there and cried and cried and cried. I have no idea how long it was before I was able to catch my breath and the lump in my throat subsided.

"Why did you have to leave me? I don't know how I'm supposed to do this without you. Every time I think I start to figure things out, like I'm finally moving in the right direction, something slaps me in the face and knocks me backwards. I need you here with me, I need you to catch me and pick me back up. You weren't supposed to leave me; we were supposed to do this together. How dare you do this to me!"

Arms wrapped around me from behind as I began to sob again, pulling me close to the masculine chest to which they belonged. I knew by the clean scent of the cologne that it was Ash, and instead of jerking away from him, I let him embrace me. He pulled me into his lap and held me close to his body while he stroked my hair and kissed my forehead. He continued to rock and soothe me in the cold darkness until I had cried out every last tear.

After I apologized and said goodbye to Evie, Ash ushered me to my car. Before closing my door, he squatted down so that he was eye level with me and reached out to brush his thumb across my cheek. "I'm really sorry for everything, Scarlett. Can we go back to one of our houses to talk about it? I can't leave things this way between us."

I nodded and agreed to talk to him at my house. I believed that he never intended to make me feel that I wasn't capable to make a decision regarding our future or that my opinion didn't matter, but his actions did just that. He needed to realize that if we were going to be together, important decisions like where we were going to go to college and live needed to be a joint discussion from the very beginning, particularly as I tried to escape that feeling of being controlled that I had lived with all of my life.

He followed me in his car for the short drive back to my house. Once we were inside, I excused myself to take a quick shower before we talked. I hadn't been home since I had left for the rehab center that morning, and especially after my bawling session, I was sure I looked like a complete mess. I quickly washed the dried mascara off of my blotchy face and then tried to scrub the funk of the day off of me under the spray of hot water. After rapidly drying myself off, I went into my room to put on something comfortable and warm. Ash was waiting for me on my bed with all kinds of pieces of paper spread out around him as well as my laptop and iPad.

"What in the world are you doing?" I asked as I grabbed my clothes.

He looked up and gave me a small smile. "I am laying out all of our options. Literally."

I couldn't help but giggle at him. I knew he felt awful and was trying to make it right, and I truly appreciated the effort. I was starting to feel bad at the way I had reacted earlier, but I had been caught completely off guard and felt like I had been deceived. However, once I had a little time to think about it, I wasn't nearly as upset as I had been. At that point I just wanted to talk about what the possibilities were so that I knew what to prepare for.

I attempted to slip my panties on while the towel was still covering me, but I clumsily fell over my own feet, and the towel ended up on the floor as did I, flat on my butt. I looked up at Ash on the bed, who was trying desperately not to laugh, and then down at myself, sprawled out naked on the floor except my panties that were half on.

"Are you sure you want to take this hot mess somewhere across the country with you?" I asked him, half joking.

"As John Legend says babe, I 'love your curves and all your edges, all your perfect imperfections,'" he answered sincerely. If I hadn't already been on the floor, I think I may have melted into a puddle on it.

"Awww that's one of the sweetest things you've ever said to me. You totally just gave me butterflies," I told him honestly as I stood up and finished pulling my panties up. I walked over to the bed and leaned down to give him a quick kiss. He groaned loudly as I pulled my away from his. "What?" I asked.

"You," he growled as he grabbed a hold of my hips and pulled me up on the bed and into his lap. "You're the hottest little thing I've ever laid my eyes on, and you're prancing around here without clothes on, knowing damn well what you're doing to me." He brought his mouth back to mine, this time giving me a much more sensual kiss.

"I'm not prancing," I mumbled against his mouth. "I'm more like flopping around."

"Well your flopping is extremely sexy, in case you didn't know," he said as he began peppering kisses up and down my neck.

"Don't think I'm not aware of what you're trying to do, Mr. Walker," I attempted to say with a stern voice, but it came out more in a breathy whisper. He was turning me into putty in his hands and completely erasing the reason I was upset to begin with.

"We are supposed to be talking about something important... I think."

"Yes, this is very important," he murmured against my sensitive skin as his head moved lower on my chest and drew a nipple into his mouth. That was all it took for me, I was a goner and all was forgiven. It was decided ~ we were moving to California.

CHAPTER FIFTEEN
Down In the Valley ~ The Head and the Heart
Can't Stop Lovin' You ~ Aerosmith (feat Carrie Underwood)

MASON

I really had no clue what to expect once I got resettled into my apartment, especially with Andi living there with me. After Scarlett left us that first evening, we both went back to our rooms and spent most of our time in there. Even though we had just been grocery shopping, the last thing I felt like doing was cooking or dirtying up the kitchen, so I just ordered some pizza and wings for us, which we both ate in the privacy of our own bedrooms. Luckily, however, it didn't feel forced or awkward with her. It wasn't like we were great friends or felt like we needed to entertain each other, we were just roommates and it was surprisingly comfortable from the very beginning.

Waking up the following morning in my apartment for the first time in months did feel a little weird. I wasn't sure what exactly to do with myself to be quite honest. I had an appointment with Heather early in the afternoon and then I was taking Andi to Empty's to introduce her to Marcus and get her set up with a job. I decided to go for a run, more to waste time than anything else. When I got back an hour or so later, Andi was lounging on the couch watching television and the house smelled of good cooking.

She looked up as I walked through the door and smiled. "Hey you," she said, her eyes drifting to the tattoo that covered my right rib cage and disappeared into my basketball shorts. Pulling her eyes back to mine, she continued, "I thought you were here so I made some breakfast, but you never came out of your room. It's in the microwave if you're hungry. It should still be warm."

"Thank you so much, you didn't have to do that, but it smells delicious," I replied with a grin. I walked directly into the kitchen and grabbed the plate of eggs, bacon, and breakfast potatoes and inhaled it in less than five minutes. I'm not sure if it tasted so damn good because I had been eating hospital food for a month and a half or due to her excellent culinary skills, but either way it was like heaven in my mouth. I washed off my plate when I had finished and loaded it in the dishwasher.

As I walked past her on my way to the shower, I complimented her. "Andi, that was amazing. Thank you again." She smiled and nodded before returning her attention to whatever she was watching on the TV.

Once I was stripped and under the spray of warm water, I exhaled a deep breath that I didn't even realize I was holding. I never realized how hard it was to simply live before; I had always just done it ~ day after day. However, the previous twenty four hours made up the longest day of my life. It was as if each minute I had to keep my mind occupied, thinking what I was going to do next. Shaking off my sudden need to over-analyze everything and anything, I quickly washed up and got dressed for my appointment with Heather.

Seeing Heather's face was a complete relief for me. Even though it was in her office instead of the rehab facility, it felt comfortable sitting across from her talking. Apparently the emotions and thoughts I had been having were completely normal because the first thing she asked me was, "Do you feel like you're living someone else's life?"

As soon as she asked, I realized that was exactly how I felt ~ like I was living a different person's life. I nodded and half-screamed at her, "Yes! That's it!"

She smiled and chuckled a bit. "That's completely normal, Mason. What you need to realize is that it's still your life, you're just looking at with a clarity that you haven't had in quite some time. Even before you began drinking and using heavily, you still had a distorted vision of not your life so much, but what was going on around you."

"So you're saying I was a self-centered asshole to everyone before?" I asked, half-joking.

"Pretty much," she answered with a grin, but I knew she was dead serious.

The rest of our appointment followed the same format as the previous ones did ~ I talked, she listened. I had never found it so easy to talk to someone before I had met her. I told her everything... things that had happened in my past, how I truly felt about everything, things I wished for the future; I held nothing back from her. She honestly wasn't overly thrilled about the Andi situation, but she said she understood why I did it. Her main concern was that if one of us relapsed, it could affect the other, but since Andi's issue was not really alcohol or drug related, she was hopeful that we could help and encourage one another.

When I got back to the apartment, I heard the shower running and was happy that Andi was already getting dressed to head up to the bar. I wanted to get there a little early to talk to Marcus. Since I was already dressed, I took the time to rest a bit on the couch and watch some mindless television. I found my thoughts drifting to Scarlett and what she was doing. I really wanted to text or call her, but I knew that wasn't my place. I had faith that she wasn't going to stop visiting now that I was out, but I couldn't help but worry that things wouldn't be quite the same. Our relationship had come a long way in the past month ~ we were actually friends now, and I really didn't want to lose that.

A little after five in the afternoon, we pulled up to the back of Empty's and I parked in my old parking spot. I kept reminding myself of what Heather had said, that I was just seeing things in a different, more selfless light. I could tell that Andi was a bit nervous as she apprehensively walked around the car and to the back door to catch up with me.

Wanting her to feel confident, I reassured her before opening the door. "Everyone is really nice here, and they're all gonna love you. Don't be surprised if they all try to make you their little sister though, okay?"

She smiled at me with those incredible blue eyes and her face lit up at my words. Seeing her dressed in fashion jeans with a snugly fitting long-sleeved top, her hair fixed and make up on, I realized how pretty she was. Her face was very young and innocent looking, almost like a little doll, and suddenly I felt protective over her. I wasn't sure exactly what her relationship was with her family, but obviously it wasn't good. I just couldn't imagine anyone not wanting to love this girl, and if one of these fuckers at the bar tried to mess with her, I'd go big brother crazy on them.

We walked through the back hallway and I pointed out the apartment, the changing rooms, and the break room before we arrived at Marcus' office. As usual he was elbows deep in paperwork and had his signature serious look on his face. I tapped on the door to alert him of our presence, and when he looked up from his desk, a smile spread across his face. He quickly stood up and walked over to us, giving me a huge bear hug, "It's so good to see you here, Rat. I've missed you."

I had never realized how much his love and support really meant to me, but after these last few months when we had really grown apart, partly because of my move to Austin and partly because I had shut him out of my life, I now knew that I both needed and wanted him to be in my life, no matter where I was. "It's good to be back, bro," I responded as I squeezed him back. "Really fucking good."

As we released each other he looked down at my tiny companion, grinning, "And you must be Andi," he said warmly and extended his hand. "I'm Marcus, this jack ass' brother and your new boss I suppose. It's a pleasure to meet you, sweetie."

She smiled brightly and put her delicate hand in his, "It's really nice to meet you, and I can't thank you enough for giving me a job. I promise I won't disappoint you."

"You are old enough to serve alcohol, right?" he asked her, half-jokingly.

Laughing, she nodded her head. "Yes, but just barely. I turned eighteen last week. Do you need my license and all of that stuff?"

"Rat boy will get you your paperwork to fill out and then show you around," he replied, looking over at me to make sure that was okay.

"Yup, come on, little one, let's finish the tour," I said, putting my arm around her shoulder. "You can fill out all the forms at the bar." I looked back at Marcus as I led her out into the main room, and his lingering smile filled me with joy.

After showing her around and introducing her to the other employees, we got all of the necessary paperwork completed just before the door opened and people slowly started trickling in. At first I had set her up to follow one of the other waitresses around, but she insisted that she could handle it on her own. I wanted to show that I had faith in her, so I agreed, but made her promise to find me if she needed any help or anyone gave her any trouble.

Several hours into the night, I came out of the office to see that the place had filled up nicely; I was excited to get back to some normalcy. I knew that 32 Leaves was going to be playing later and I was hoping to get a chance to talk to Max. We had been pretty good friends when I had first met Scarlett and he was dating Evie, and with everything that had happened last year, I really just wanted to clear the air with him. I headed in the direction of their usual table and was relieved to see him sitting there .

"Hey, Max," I said as I walked up. All of the heads at the table turned to look at me, and I cringed internally knowing what they were all thinking. I took a deep breath, shook it off, and smiled at all of them. I nodded my head at the rest of the table. "Mina... Noah... guys... good to see you all." Everyone said hello, but I could feel the tension in the air.

Mina, God love her sweet soul, came over and gave me a hug, making me feel a little better. "It's good to see you back, Mase. You had us all a little worried."

I smiled meekly. "Yeah, well I'm getting back on track now... just a little derailment. Thank you though, and I'm really sorry about the wed..."

"Shh! No need to apologize. Just promise me you aren't gonna do anything stupid again," she interrupted me.

Chuckling, I said, "I can't promise I won't do *anything* stupid, but I'm not getting mixed up in that shit again. I've got too much to live for."

"Good, that's what I want to hear," she replied as she walked back over to her barstool.

Just as I was going to ask Max to talk for a minute alone, Andi walked up to the table. "Good evening, guys. What can I get you to drink?" I watched as she made her way around the table, getting each of their orders, ready to pounce if any of them made a lewd remark towards her. Luckily for them, they were all very respectful, but I couldn't help but notice the way she and Max looked at each other when they interacted, almost as if they knew each other. I made a mental note to ask her about it when we got back to the apartment later.

When she walked away to the bar to get their drinks, one of the guys asked, "Who's the new waitress, Rat? Are y'all recruiting at the local high schools now?"

"Shut the fuck up, dude," Max barked before I even had a chance to say anything. I cocked my head at him, now really interested in what was going on, but I refrained from saying anything there.

"Alright, alright. Shit, I was just saying she looks like she's fifteen," the guy responded, putting his hands up in the air to surrender.

"Well, I'm sure she's old enough to work here. Marcus and Rat don't run a shady business." He looked over at me, "Right, man?"

I nodded. "Yes, she's legal, and yes, Marcus runs a tight ship. This place ain't mine anymore, I'm just here for a few weeks until I head back to Austin." I paused a minute before asking him, "Actually, do you have a few minutes to talk before y'all go on?" He agreed and we walked over to the end of the bar where we had some privacy and could hear a little better.

"Look, I don't want to make this long and drawn out, but I just wanted to tell you that I really miss having you as a friend. I know a lot of shit has happened. We've both made some pretty fucking stupid decision and reacted poorly to things. I'm sorry I hit you at the wedding," I said sincerely. Making things right between people

I had once cared about was a huge part of my self-forgiveness process, which was vital in the whole self-love thing.

He took a minute, digesting my words before he responded. "You're completely right. We both did some things that we shouldn't be proud of. I want you to know that I deserved that punch though; it's why I didn't even try to defend myself. I could give you a thousand excuses for what I did, but none of them mean shit. All I can say is I'm sorry... really fucking sorry. You have no idea how badly I'd like to redo that night." He shook his head remorsefully.

"I get it. You don't need to say anything else. Believe me, I know more than anyone. I just wanted things to be cool between us. Like I said earlier, I'm gonna be around here for a little while before heading back to Austin, and I'd love sometime in the future for Jobu's Rum and 32 Leaves to play together again." I felt such a relief that this conversation was going so smoothly.

"Yeah, I wanted to talk to you about that," he began cautiously. "As you know..." He suddenly stopped what he was saying as something behind me caught his eye. Naturally, I turned around to see what or who it was, and immediately my eyes found Scarlett walking through the front door... followed by Ash.

SCARLETT

The day after my and Ash's argument, and subsequent make up, we spent quite a bit of time talking about and planning for our upcoming move. Once we had the chance to discuss everything in detail, I began to get excited. UC Berkeley had an award winning College of Music so it was really a perfect fit for both of us. I had never dreamed of living in California before, and I wasn't sure how my parents were going to feel about me leaving Rice, an academic mecca, for a music school on the west coast, but I had to remind myself that I wasn't living this life for them.

We still needed to figure out where we were going to live, but we decided that we would go at the end of May, as soon as the semester was over. Ash had a job through the school doing research, similar to what he had at St. Thomas, and I would try to find one once we got out there. He kept telling me that it wasn't necessary for me to work, that he could pay for everything, but I wanted to be able to help with our living expenses, even if he didn't need it. I explained to him that if I didn't, I felt like I was completely dependent on him, which of course was what I was trying to escape. Thankfully, he finally got it, and told me that he supported whatever made me happy.

That evening I was singing with 32 Leaves for the first time at Empty's, and I was both excited and nervous. After Max had talked to Noah and the rest of the band, they had welcomed me with open arms. I quickly learned that singing with a band was much different than what I was used to, just me and my guitar or keyboard, but after practicing with them a few times, I finally felt confident enough to perform.

Max had left while I was still getting ready, saying that he had some errands to run before heading up to the bar. Ash had gone home to shower and get dressed and was coming back to pick me up. I think he was just as excited to see me with the band as I was to perform with them. I dressed in a black V-neck sweater with skinny jeans and black knee boots, hoping for a good mixture of comfort and style. As I finished straightening my hair and putting on a small bit of makeup, I found myself really wishing Evie was there. Not only was she my personal stylist, but she had always been my biggest fan. Just her presence had a calming sensation that no one or nothing else could rival.

A little after nine o'clock, Ash and I walked in and headed straight for the table where Max, Noah, Mina, and the rest of the band always sat. As we walked across the room, I noticed that Max's chair was empty so my eyes began scanning the room. It didn't take me long to find him. His eyes locked with mine, pleading, and I immediately knew why. I hadn't even thought about seeing Mase up there; it had just never occurred to me that while he was still in Houston, that he would be there. He turned around and followed Max's line of sight, and when our eyes locked, the nervous butterflies in my belly turned into a wild zoo.

CHAPTER SIXTEEN
Hesitate ~ Stone Sour
Let Her Go ~ Passenger

MASON

I knew it had only been the day before that I had seen her, but I could not take my eyes off of her. She was absolutely stunning. Max stepped up behind me and quietly whispered in my ear, "Dude, you're staring."

"I'm well aware. I can't help it, look at her," I replied.

"Yes, I see her. And I also see her boyfriend walking behind her," he chuckled.

With a half groan, I forced myself to pull my gaze away from her and turn back around to face Max. Rubbing my face to try and get the image of her out of my head, I asked him, "So what were you about to say?"

He gave me a crooked smile. "Well, I was going to warn you that she was coming."

I was a little confused because Scarlett never mentioned coming up to the bar anymore, and I couldn't imagine that Ash liked to hang out there much. "Does she come up here a lot?"

"No, she's actually singing with 32 Leaves tonight."

"What? Why? What's wrong with Noah?"

"Nothing's wrong with him, he's still our main guy. She was wanting to get back into music, and we were looking for a way to diversify our set, so she's just gonna do a few songs with us. Tonight is our first night live with her," he explained. "She's really fucking good, man."

"So that's why he's here with her," I muttered, as it all began to make sense.

Max put his hand on my shoulder, his eyes understanding. "He truly loves her; he'd do anything for her."

As I nodded and swiveled on my heel to walk away, I mumbled under my breath, "So do I... so do I." I needed some fresh air and a minute to calm down before greeting the cute couple, so I hurried to the back door before they reached us. Standing outside in the freezing cold night without a jacket, I began counting backwards from ten to calm myself and regain my composure. As simple as it may sound, I found that the anger control technique helped me quite a bit when my thoughts began to run away from me.

Startling me, the door swung open, nearly knocking me over, and Scarlett stepped outside. My heart soared knowing she had come looking for me, I didn't even realize she had seen me escape.

"Mase! What are you doing out here? Why did you run when you saw me?" I could hear the hurt in her voice.

"I just needed a minute, Angel. I'm okay. I'm not out here doing lines or anything," I said, in an attempt to make light of the situation.

She slapped me hard across the back of the head. "Don't you even joke about that, Mason Templeton. I will kick your ass."

"Ouch, that hurt!" I cried as I rubbed that back of my head. "I was only kidding."

"Now why did you come out here when I got here? Are you trying to avoid me?"

"I would never try to avoid you. I just wasn't expecting you to be here... and him," I ran my fingers through my overgrown hair. "I know what the situation is, Scar, and I accept it, but it doesn't make it any easier, okay? I'm trying here. "

She stepped towards me, eliminating the space between us, and circled her arms around my waist and leaning her forehead onto my shoulder. Instinctively, I wrapped my arms around her and pulled her close to me. Her scent reminded me of a warm night on the beach, the fresh air mixed with a hint of ocean sea breeze and coconuts. I tried desperately not to think about how she tastes as good as she smells, but it's nearly impossible with her this close to me.

Without looking up, she whispered, "Mase, I thought we were moving forward as friends. You don't run away from your friends. Like I've told you, I want you in my life, and I want to be in yours. I can't even begin to tell you how important you are to me, but I'm with him now... whatever the messed up circumstances that brought us here, it's where we are."

Gently stroking her back with my hands, I knew what she said was true. I knew I had to let her go in that capacity. As much as I fucking didn't want to, I was going to go insane like that. I knew it was part of moving forward and learning to love myself. I kissed the top of her head. "I'll be okay, Angel. Just be patient with me. Now let's go back inside. I want to hear you sing."

She pulled back from me a bit, looking down at the ground, and said, "Wait, there's something I need to tell you first." She chewed on her lip nervously, obviously deciding how she was going to say whatever it was that she needed to say.

I put my hand under her chin and lifted her face so that she was looking into my eyes. "What is it? Just say it."

"Ash and I are moving to California in May, after the semester is over," she blurted out.

There haven't been many times in my life that I've been speechless, but that was one. I was literally stunned silent. I dropped my hand from her chin and put them in my pockets and just stood there staring at her.

I could see the tears forming in her eyes as she tried to explain further. "Please don't be upset with me. I'm gonna go to music school there and he's gonna finish graduate school. I mean you're leaving to go back to Austin here in a couple of weeks, and from there you're probably going to be on tour. You'll be long gone before I ever leave."

I knew she was right in everything she said. I would be leaving Houston in just a short time, but for some reason knowing that she was not only moving in with him, but moving across the country with him, made me extremely jealous. I swallowed down the lump that had formed in my throat as I gazed down at her. One single tear fell down her cheek, and I reached up to wipe it off with a gentle stroke of my thumb. I knew in that moment that I had to let her go. She needed me to tell her it was okay, and as much as it killed me to do so, I did just that.

"I wish you the best, Angel. I know you'll be amazing at anything you do," I said with a forced smile, as I fought my own tears. "I'll always be your biggest fan and you will always have a special place in my heart. I can never thank you enough for your love and support... for always believing in me. Anytime you need me, for any reason, I will be there for you."

"We aren't saying goodbye yet. We will still see each other before you leave?" Her words were more of a question than a statement.

"Yes, but who knows if we'll get another chance to be alone. I just wanted you to know... this way when I do leave, we don't have to do the sad goodbye. Okay?"

She gave me her best fake smile, and as desperately as I wanted to pull her back into my arms and kiss her full lips, even if it was for one last time, I didn't. Neither of us said anything else, we went back inside the bar and each went our separate ways ~ her to the table with Ash, Mina, Max and the rest of 32 Leaves while I went to find and check on Andi.

SCARLETT

When I returned to the table, I could feel the inquisitive eyes on me. I was sure they saw Mason and I come in the back door together, but I was at the point that I didn't give two shits what everyone else thought. I sat down next to Ash and he put his hand on my thigh, squeezing it for comfort. He knew what I had just done, and he understood that it wasn't easy for me. I gave him a quick peck on the lips and a look that said we would talk about it later. Max gave me a look that told me he was completely lost on what was going on, but as soon as the waitress approached the table, his attention was drawn to her.

"Can I get you anything to drink, Scarlett?" I heard a sweet female voice ask.

Confused on how the waitress knew my name, I looked up to meet those same crystal blue eyes that I was introduced to the day before. "Andi!" I exclaimed, remembering that Mase had said he was getting her a job. She leaned in and gave me a quick hug before asking me if I wanted anything to drink again.

As she walked away, both Ash and Max asked in unison, "Who is that?" I laughed, looking back and forth between the two of them. "That's Andi, she's Mason's new roommate. I picked them both up from the center yesterday and took them to his apartment.

Max crinkled his forehead in displeasure, "Are they together?"

I shook my head. "No, not that I know of or that was evident yesterday. From what I could gather, she doesn't have any family so he offered her a place to stay and a job. Her issues are..." I struggled to find the right word without spreading her business to others. "Different. She's got different problems than Mason," I explained vaguely.

Thankfully, Noah interrupted us, letting us know that it was time to take the stage. Suddenly my belly filled with nervous butterflies, I really hoped I was ready for this. I kissed Ash before joining the rest of the band, waiting for Noah to introduce me. As soon as I took the microphone in my hands, I forgot about everyone and everything but the music; it was just me and the band in my world for those four songs.

When I was finished with my part of their performance, I hopped down off the stage and made my way back to where Ash and Mina were sitting. I knew the smile on my face stretched from ear to ear and I felt like I was floating. God, I felt amazing. The beats were still thumping through my body, in the same pattern as my heart was beating, and the adrenaline coursing through my veins was exhilarating. They both stood up to hug and congratulate me when I reached the table. Ash picked me and swung me around, whispering in my ear, "I'm so proud of you, Scarlett. You were absolutely incredible."

We sat there to watch the rest of 32 Leaves' performance, and several other people, including Andi, stopped by to tell me that I did a great job. I was seriously on cloud nine... I only wished Mase would've come by to say something too, but I understood why he didn't.

After the guys finished up, they all re-joined us for a celebratory round of beers and they all bought me shots, saying that it was part of the initiation process. Spirits were high, we all knew that we had nailed it, and I had three shots down when I heard that familiar voice come through over the speakers.

"Evenin' folks. I, uh... I'm not used to being up here by myself. I'm Mason, for those who don't know me." Some girl interrupted him, yelling out, "We've missed you, Rat!" He laughed, "Or Rat, if you prefer. The rest of Jobu's Rum is in Austin, but I'm here a few weeks, so I thought I'd play a song or two."

I heard him rustling around and getting ready, but I didn't look up. I knew that Ash and Max were watching me, and that combined with the liquor that I had just consumed, had my face burning. I desperately wanted to get up and walk outside. I had no idea what he was going to sing, but I didn't want to stick around to find out. However, I also knew that if I left, it would make even more of a scene, so I just sat there staring at the beer on the table in front of me.

He strummed the guitar a few times, making sure it was in tune before he began. As soon as he played the opening chords, I hissed in a breath of air between my teeth as my heart plummeted into my stomach, realizing the song he was playing was indeed for me. I was frozen in place, my eyes still fixated on the amber liquid in the glass in front of me, my throat had a golf ball-sized sob lodged into it, and my heart at a dead standstill; every word he sang ripped deeper and deeper into my soul. The entire bar was silent, watching him in awe, as he performed the song better than the original artist, his voice saturated with sadness and sorrow. As he whispered the last "And you let her go," I finally pulled my gaze up to look at him. He was staring directly at me and then said in a low whisper the five words that cut me deeper than I ever thought possible. "I'm letting you go, Angel."

CHAPTER SEVENTEEN
Beneath Your Beautiful ~ Labrinth (feat Emeli Sandi)
It Won't Stop ~ Sevyn Streeter (feat Chris Brown)

ASH

I should've gotten some kind of fucking award for sitting there listening to him sing to her. If it had been any other song other than one with him telling her goodbye, I probably would've gone all caveman and thrown Scarlett over my shoulder, hauling her ass out of there. It still killed me because I knew that he was upsetting her, but I also knew that she had just told him about our moving. I tried to put myself in his shoes, and I gave him his chance to say goodbye. I hoped he truly realized that he had blown his shot with her, and now that she was mine, I wasn't ever letting her go.

As soon as the song was over, I put my hand on the small of her back and leaned in to her ear, whispering, "Are you ready to go or do you want to stay?"

She didn't say a word; she just hopped off her bar stool, grabbed her purse, and began walking towards the exit. I said a blanket goodbye to the table and followed after her. I wasn't sure what to expect when I finally caught up to her. Honestly, I expected tears and a pretty foul mood, but when I finally reached her waiting by the car, she seemed to be fine. I still proceeded with caution. I wasn't sure if I should bring up anything or not. I went with not.

We got in the car and she began talking about her performance and things that she needed to work on. I of course told her I thought she was amazing, because well... I did. She then started talking about what classes she wanted to take in the fall at UC Berkeley. It made me happy that she seemed excited about the upcoming move; I had this amazing feeling that everything was happening the way it was supposed to.

When we got back to her apartment, Scarlett took a quick shower while I prepared us both a grilled cheese sandwich and a glass of milk for a midnight snack. I had it waiting for her on a tray in bed when she got out. I loved seeing her eyes light up with joy at little things that I did for her. That alone was payment enough for pampering her for the rest of our lives.

"Thank you so much! I was just thinking how hungry I was," she said as she sat down and leaned over to give me a kiss.

"You're more than welcome. I figured you would be; I noticed that you didn't eat much dinner earlier, and then the beer and those shots..."

"Ugh, yes. Please don't remind me." She picked up one of the warm cheesy triangles and took a big bite, then chased it with a big gulp of the ice cold milk. "Mmmm... there is really nothing better. How can this not put someone in a good mood?"

Shrugging, I followed suit, devouring my sandwich in less than five minutes. "I don't know," I said as I wiped the crumbs off of my mouth with a napkin. "That's the ultimate comfort food. All it needed was a little bacon."

She nodded as she popped the last bite in her mouth. "Yessss... bacon makes everything better."

"Next time I'll make them with bacon." I kissed the tip of her nose before taking the tray with the empty plates back to the kitchen.

It was my turn for a quick shower, which I did in record speed so that I could join her in bed. She was sitting up watching House Hunters on HGTV when I slid under the covers next to her. I laughed softly at her obsession with that damn show. "Haven't you seen this one before?" I teased her.

She crinkled her nose up at me. "No, I haven't, smart ass." She turned her head back to the television. "And this is a good one, it's the international version and they are buying a house in Puerto Rico."

I pulled her into my lap so that I could rub her back and shoulders while she finished watching the show. As I massaged her lower back, I leaned in to press my lips to the back of her neck. Her clean coconut scent was intoxicating, and I couldn't help but kiss my way over to her earlobe, nibbling on it a bit. The slight moan that escaped her lips and the goose bumps that covered her skin gave me the green light to continue. I continued to kiss her neck as my hands moved from her back around to her belly, slipping underneath the hem of her shirt. My hands slowly crept up her ribcage until my thumb swept across the swell of her breast.

"Which house do you think they're going to pick?" I asked in a breathy whisper against her ear.

She slightly arched her back, pressing her chest into my hand. "I think they'll get house number two," she mumbled.

I quickly had both nipples in between my thumbs and forefingers, tugging and twisting gently. "You think so? I think they may get house number three," I said without even looking up at the television.

After several minutes of kissing every square inch of the back of her neck and caressing her boobs and nipples, I began to walk my fingers back down her belly until I was tracing the elastic edge of her panties. Groaning, I slid my fingers inside the waistband, softly running it back and forth along the soft flesh of her lower abdomen. Continuing to move my hands further south, my fingertips quickly found her already damp folds. Gently parting her lips with my fingers, I began to lazily trace a circular pattern around her clit. She leaned her head back on to my shoulder, eyes closed, and lifted her hips into my touch. My cock was pressing into her back and I growled when she arched and pushed her tight little ass up against it.

I shoved her panties to the side, gliding my fingers through the wet, sticky nectar and dragging it up to coat her swollen clit. I could see her bite down on her bottom lip as she began to squirm under my hand. Increasing the rhythm of my fingers, her whimpers turned into pleas, and I was unable to resist her cries any longer. I moved my hand down to her tight slit, first delving one finger, and then another deep into her core. Slowly, I moved my fingers in and out of her, rubbing her inner wall with each thrust while pushing my thumb against her hardened nub. I could feel her clenching down on my hand as her orgasm drew near.

Not wanting her to cum quite yet, I suddenly removed my hand from her panties. Her eyes shot open and she turned around to look at me, partially confused and even more frustrated. "Why did you do that?" she whined.

I leaned down and took her bottom lip in my mouth and suck on it gently. Mumbling against her mouth, I said, "Trust me." I brought my fingers to her mouth, covered in her sweet juices and tapped her lips to get her to open up. I could see the internal struggle in her face. Part of her wanted to, the mere thought turned her on, but she also felt like she shouldn't want to taste herself on my hand. I looked at her straight in the eye and again I said, "Trust me."

She parted her lips and drew my fingers in her mouth, sucking them clean for me. When she had finished, my mouth crashed down on hers, getting my own taste of her sweetness from her mouth. I was intoxicated by the smell of her desire that hung heavy in the air, and the tiny little taste that I had of her was only enough to initiate my hunger. I needed my mouth on her. I needed to show her that she had made the right choice.

SCARLETT

I wasn't sure how we went from a back massage to a full on
sexual onslaught of my entire body, but I can't say that I minded
much either. The night at the bar had been a total roller coaster. I
went from being at the top of the world after performing to picking
up the pieces of my heart on the floor after Mason did. I felt like a
bottle of nerves that had been shaken to the point of explosion. I
needed something to make me forget about the real world; I
needed a release.

After teasing me to the brink with his fingers, Ash slid out from
behind me and propped me up against the pillow. I was in a
trance, completely mesmerized by his movements, craving his next
touch. He hovered over me as his mouth came crashing down on
to lips, his tongue demanding entrance and then slowly rolled
against mine. Pulling his mouth from me, he began to kiss his way
down my chin, my neck, and my chest; his wet lips leaving a trail
of tingles over my skin. Hastily, he grabbed the bottom of my shirt
and pulled it up and over my head, leaving my breasts completely
exposed. I heard him growl as he immediately brought his mouth
down on my chest, his tongue tracing the perimeter of the
darkened skin, then his tongue darting out to flick over the
pebbled nipple. His hand had a hold of the other boob, massaging
it with his fingers and rolling my nipple under his thumb.

My hand fell to his cheek, caressing the side of his face, as my
breathing became labored. A low fire started to burn deep in my
belly, causing my legs to wrap around his hips, pressing up against
my body. He looked up at me and laughed, "What house did they
choose, Butterfly?"

I grabbed the back of his head and pressed his face back in my
chest and said, "I'm not sure. I think house number two" He
muttered something against my skin that sounded like "I bet it was
house number three," but I wasn't quite sure and really didn't
care. It was taking all of the patience I had not to push his head
straight down in between my legs. The aching in my core was
increasing rapidly, I needed to be touched there quickly.

As he began to move down my body again, my body began to
shake in anticipation. "Please...oh please," I begged him to hurry.
He looked up with a smirk on his face and shook his head. "I said
to trust me. I promise I will take care of you."

He continued his shimmy downward, dipping his tongue in my
belly button as he passed over it. Then , finally he reached my
panties. I felt his fingers hook on the sides on them one moment,

and the next I heard a rip and I was completely naked in front of him. Without thought my hips lifted off of the bed towards his face, eager for his oral assault. He splayed one hand across my tummy, forcing me back on the bed, and then put his face just inches from my sweet spot. I can feel his warm breath against my sensitive skin just before he begins to lightly kiss my already soaked lips. Using his other hand to spread my folds, he leisurely licked up and down the delicate flesh; my body trembling underneath him. He moved his mouth up to my clit, where he had already teased me to no end with his fingers, and began sucking gently on it as his tongue swirled around it.

I grabbed at the sheets next to me, bunching them into tight balls in my palm as I try desperately to control myself. When he moved his mouth down and plunges his tongue deep inside me, I couldn't help but writhe under him. I turned my face towards the pillow, muffling out the moans that are falling from my lips, as I unashamedly ground my pussy against his mouth and chin. Completely inebriated with lust, the room went dark as I shut my eyes and lost myself to the sensuality and passion that he wreaked upon my body. Alternating his mouth and fingers from my clit to my core, I began to unravel as the slow burn morphed into a white hot inferno coursing through my veins. He pulled my clit into his mouth one last time, allowing his teeth to graze over it, just as he thrust his fingers inside of me, curling them and pressing hard on my gspot. I couldn't hold on any longer; I fell off the cliff and allowed the ecstasy to consume my body. My back shot up off the bed, my walls began contracting around his fingers, and I screamed out, "Fuuuccckkkk!" so loud the neighbors surely heard. He continued to hold and kiss me as I came back to reality, my legs quivering and my body completely flushed.

I felt him crawl back up my body so that his face was even with mine, even though my eyes were closed. "Open your eyes, butterfly," he commanded softly. I obeyed his wish and opened my eyes, staring directly into his. He ran his fingertip lightly down the side of my face, from my forehead to my chin as he murmured, "Watching you cum is so fucking beautiful."

His words sent a fluttering in my belly, and I desperately wanted to return the favor for him. I turned my face into his touch, taking his finger in my mouth as he had asked me to do earlier, and sucked my juices off of them. He watched my mouth as I cleaned his hand, and then pressed his forehead to mine with his eyes closed, groaning. "What am I going to do with you?"

I rolled our bodies so that he was on his back and I was straddling his waist. "I don't know," I answered. "But I know what I'm going to do with you." And just as he had begun, I started placing kisses on his mouth, then his chin, and down his neck, working my way down his body. Just before I took off his boxers off with my teeth, I looked up his body and said, "They definitely got house number two."

CHAPTER EIGHTEEN
Say Something ~ A Great Big World (feat Christina Aguilara)
Can't Help Falling in Love ~ Ingrid Michaelson
Which Way Your Heart Will Go ~ Mason Jennings

MASON

If I thought the first night in my apartment was hard, the second night damn near killed me. After closing up the bar, Andi and I didn't get home until nearly three o'clock in the morning. After a nice hot shower, I crawled into bed hoping to fall fast asleep, but despite my body being completely exhausted, my brain refused to stop. I couldn't stop thinking about Scarlett and everything that had transpired over the evening. I was moving back to Austin, she was moving to California, and we were both moving forward with our lives, searching for our euphoria, just without each other.

The last month with her had really been bittersweet. I had gotten to know her on such a personal level during her visits, and I loved her even more than I once did. That was why letting her go this time was so hard. I knew that she would always be there for me if I ever needed anything and that she would support me in everything, but I also knew that that with her moving away, the distance between us would lead to us not talking as much and seeing each other even less.

Groaning, I rolled over for what seemed like the thousandth time that night, still unable to find dream land. A soft knock at the door startled me. Knowing it had to be Andi, and hoping nothing was wrong, I called out, "Come on in."

The door slowly opened and she tiptoed in, looking adorable in her footed pajamas. She really was like a big kid. "I can't sleep, and I heard you in here, so I thought maybe we could keep each other company."

Smiling, I scooted over and patted the bed. "Jump in, kiddo. What's on your mind? Why can't you sleep?"

She quickly climbed up on the bed and sat cross-legged, looking at me. Shrugging her shoulders, she looked down at her leg and began picking invisible fuzz off of it. "I dunno. I've had insomnia since before I can remember. I get in my own head too much. What about you? Why are you awake?"

"Same. I'm too much in my head tonight, or this morning I guess I should say," as I looked at the alarm clock that read five thirty.

"Can I ask you a personal question?" she asked.

I chuckled. "You can ask, but I can't guarantee that I'll answer."

"What's the deal between you and Scarlett? I mean I know I just met y'all and all but it all seems kinda bizarre. She picked us up on Saturday and I thought y'all were like best friends or something, but then I noticed she got a little weird when we were here at the apartment. And then tonight... I don't even know where to start. She shows up with another guy, the two of y'all disappear out back for a while, you both go separate ways when you come back in, she sings, you sing, you look at her and tell her you're letting her go, you break her heart, and then she leaves with other guy." I looked at her in astonishment. How in the world did she pick up on all of that? "Did I miss anything? I think that just about summed it up," she grinned, proud of herself. "Oh wait, and you both obviously know some really hot guy, cause I saw you talking to him and he sat next to her at the table.

"Well, Miss Smarty Pants, I guess you don't need me to answer since you've got it all figured out," I retorted, flipping her hair playfully.

"No, I know what happened, now I want to know why it happened."

"Ugh..." I grumbled. "Okay, short story. Scarlett and I used to be together, we lived here together for a while. We had a huge misunderstanding and broke up; however, once we realized it was just a misunderstanding, it was too late. Words had been said, things had been done... it was just too much. But while I was in rehab, she started coming to visit, just as a good friend, and we've actually gotten even closer. She told me tonight she and her boyfriend, Ash, are moving to California in a few months."

"But aren't you moving away soon too?"

"Yes, but I'll still come visit here. It's only a couple hours driving, and seeing her a little was better than nothing. Now she's gonna be on the other side of the country..."

"Ah, I see," she said as she leaned over to give me a quick hug. "So you still love her?"

"There will never be a day that I don't," I admitted.

"Then why'd you let her go? Why not fight for her?"

"I felt like it was the right thing to do. As much as it's not what I really want to do, I know it's time to move on.

"I've never been in love, so I have no idea what that feels like, but I'm sure it sucks ass."

Laughing hard at her choice of words, I agreed. "Yes, it pretty much sucks ass.

"What? I think it's a great description," she huffed. "Now tell me about your cute friend."

"Who? The guy you kept making googoo eyes at tonight" I teased, happy to divert the conversation elsewhere.

She slapped my shoulder, but was laughing as well. "I did not make googoo eyes at him. I was just admiring his overall hotness. Now what's his name and why didn't you introduce me?

"His name is Max and I didn't introduce you because I had a weird feeling that y'all already knew each other. I thought that was the reason for the eyes."

"Shut up about the eyes!" she yelled, her face was pink from the blush that had crept up her neck. "Tell me more about him!"

I couldn't help but crack up at her attempt to deny the faces she was making at him all night. When I finally stopped laughing, I told her a little bit about Max... all I could without bringing up Evie. She also made me promise to introduce her the next time he was there, which I agreed to do. Even after what had happened with Scarlett, if there was any guy that I would've picked for Andi to hang out with, it would be Max, and it appeared that in a few short months, they would be the only ones still in town. I felt I could trust him to watch over her when I was gone, even if he still wasn't ready for any type of romantic relationship.

~   ~   ~   ~   ~

The next several weeks flew by quickly. Part of me was eager to get back to Austin ~ to my friends there and to making music; I couldn't wait to get Jobu's Rum up and going again. I had so much music that I had written while I was gone, and I couldn't wait to hear it all put together. However, there was a part of me that was a little sad about leaving. Andi had proven to be a great roommate, but an even better friend. She truly was like a little sister to me. I had only had one night since being out of rehab that I was really tempted to drink, and she sat and talked me through it for hours. She didn't leave my side until I was asleep in my bed.

I had introduced her to Max as promised just days after our first conversation about him. I knew that she was crushing on him hard, but she played it cool when she was around him. I knew he had really taken a liking to her too, but it was hard for him. I had asked him to keep an eye on her and the apartment while I was gone, and he was more than eager to comply. She was still reluctant to talk about her family much, but I didn't press the issue. I knew that she would when she was good and ready. In addition, I wasn't sure she knew about the Evie situation either. I didn't say a word about it; that was Max's story to tell when he felt it was necessary. I realized I wasn't the only one that noticed their flirting when one night up at Empty's, I overheard Mina tell Max, "Just fuck her already, y'all are making me throw up in my mouth with that sweet shit." I laughed to myself because not only did I agree, but Mina always had such an eloquent way with words.

Scarlett became a regular up at the bar again ever since she started singing with the band. Ash would come with her on the weekends, but during the week she would always come with Max. We still continued to text occasionally, and the times she was there without Ash we would sit and talk about everything, much like we did during her center visits. When he was with her, she never ignored me or anything like that, but I understood why he wouldn't be cool with her just coming over to hang out with me. Shit, I wouldn't want her talking to me at all if I was him, but that was just the possessive asshole in me, I guessed. I did try to be mindful and not overtly flirt with her or make her uncomfortable in any way. I was quickly learning that respect was a two way street; I needed to give to receive, and there was a way to respect yourself without being selfish.

I also continued to see Heather twice a week during the six weeks after my release. She was an incredible therapist, and I was a bit worried about what I was going to do without her. I tried many times to talk her into setting up a practice in Austin; I begged, pleaded, and even used bribery tactics. Unfortunately, she wouldn't budge. I did schedule a monthly appointment to drive in and see her, just to keep her up to speed with everything that was going on, and well, because I just liked her.

One day when I was leaving her office, I thought to myself, "I am great friends with three absolutely gorgeous women, and I'm not having sex with any of them." As a matter of fact, I wasn't having sex at all! It had been close to four months since I had been with anyone, and even though my hand was getting pretty damn tired of taking care of business, I didn't have much desire. I wasn't attracted to the idea of a quick fuck in the back of the bar like I used to do regularly, I didn't feel comfortable bringing home some strange girl to the apartment with Andi there, and since I knew I wasn't staying, I wasn't interested in looking for anyone to date regularly. Wow, what a three-sixty my life had taken in the matter of just a year.

Before I knew it, it was the first weekend of April and it was time for me to go. Marcus and I had a nice talk prior to my leaving where he wished me the best and promised to make it up for one of my shows in Austin. Andi refused to let me get emotional as I hugged her tightly and told her that I promised to be back soon. She told me not to worry about her or the apartment and kissed me on the cheek as I left. Just before getting on my bike to make the three hour journey westward, I sent Scarlett two text message.

> **ME: Wise men say only fools rush in...I'd be your fool over and over again. Never regret.**

> **ME: Don't stop until you find your euphoria, Angel.**

I didn't wait to see if she would respond; I stuck my phone in my jacket pocket and took off down the road.

SCARLETT

I was having brunch with Ash and his mom when the goodbye texts from Mase came through on my phone. It took everything in me to not start crying, but I didn't. I just put my phone back in my purse and forced myself to focus on the conversation we were having. I knew Robin still wasn't completely over me up and leaving the Christmas dinner, even though Ash had assured me that she loved me and understood why I had done it. I would reply to him later.

I still couldn't believe it was already April. Ash and I were set and ready to move over Memorial Day weekend the following month. The closer that it got, the more I excited I became. Not only had I had never lived in another state before, but Ash and I would officially be living together. Even though we spent many nights together already, we were still pretty strict in our weekday schedules at our own places so that we could focus on school and work. I had begun performing with 32 Leaves on a regular basis twice a week as well, so it gave me time to practice with them on our off days.

After the night Mase had told me that he was letting me go, Ash and I had yet another serious conversation about my relationship with him. I was honest as I could be about my feelings. I told him that I loved Mason, and would always have a special place in my heart, but he was my past and Ash was my future. Mase and I would continue to be friends; I had told him that I would be there for him if he ever needed me, but I would never do anything to jeopardize my relationship with Ash, and he knew that. Part of me thought that Ash just agreed with it because he knew that we would be going our separate ways soon enough and he wouldn't have to worry about me seeing him anymore. Either way, I valued the last couple of months that I had with Mason before he moved. When we didn't cloud our relationship with sex and the stress of outside forces, we were great friends. I was incredibly proud of him for taking control of his life and getting back on track. Heather was a huge reason for that, and I was so thankful that she had come in his life when she did. Honestly, there was a tiny sliver of worry in me about him regressing when he moved back to Austin, but I held strong to my faith in him.

When we got back in the car after leaving Robin's condo, Ash grabbed my hand and squeezed it. "I know and it's okay," he said compassionately.

I turned to look at him and smiled. Sometimes it was creepy how in tune he was with my feelings. "You always know and I'll be okay."

"He's right, ya know? You really are an angel."

"Oh, hush," I retorted. "I'm far from that."

"You saved me from the path of misery that I was on. Before I met you, I just did a lot of things to make me feel good so that I didn't have to deal with the demons inside of me. It's the same thing with him. We both want to be better people for you."

I reached up and cupped his face with my hands, staring intently into his beautiful blue eyes. "I want you both to be better people for yourselves. Evie should've taught us all that we aren't guaranteed tomorrow. If I was no longer here, I want to know that you would both continue to be the best people that you can. That's what I'm striving for now ~ to be the best me I can be. And when that happens, then everything else will fall in place." I leaned over and planted a gentle kiss on his lips. "I love you, Ash Walker, and I can't wait to be the best us for the rest of our lives."

His smile warmed my heart as he kissed me on the forehead before starting the car and heading home.

CHAPTER NINETEEN
Come Away With Me ~ Norah Jones
Unbroken ~ Demi Lovato

ASH

Moving day was finally upon us. Excited couldn't even begin to express how I felt when I woke up that morning. Thrilled... overjoyed... exhilarated... those didn't do it justice either. I got out of bed almost an hour before the alarm clock ever went off; I just couldn't lie there any longer. I had said my goodbyes to Jess and Meg the night before which had been both a cry fest and full of laughs. I was really going to miss those girls; they had been my roommates for over four years and I loved them like my sisters. They were going to continue to live in my house and pay the rent to my mom. My room was going to remain empty so when we did come back to visit, we had a place to stay.

After quickly throwing on some khaki shorts, a t-shirt, and my flip flops, I grabbed the one suitcase that I was taking and headed out the door. I stopped and picked up doughnuts and coffee on my way to Scarlett's apartment to help bribe her out of bed. I had no doubt that she was still snug and cozy under her covers. Letting myself in with my key, I wasn't surprised at all to see Andi asleep on the couch. Ever since Mason had gone back to Austin, she had become a somewhat permanent fixture at Scarlett and Max's apartment. She and Scarlett had become good friends and I wasn't sure what was going on between her and Max. It was evident to everyone in the world that they were perfect for each other, but something kept holding them back. My guess was Max's guilt over Evie, but anytime I tried bringing it up with him, he would quickly change the subject. Nonetheless, we had all taken her in to our circle because she was downright adorable and the sweetest thing.

Andi opened her eyes as I closed the door behind me. "Morning, Andi girl, I brought breakfast," I greeted her.

She sat up with a big grin on her face. "Good morning, Ash. It smells delish, thank you. Are you all ready to go?"

I nodded as I walked her over a coffee. "You have no idea," I said as I tousled her bed hair. "Not that I'm not gonna miss you guys... but you know what I mean."

"Of course I do. I'd be excited too. Don't worry about me and Max, we will just hold down the fort here on the Gulf Coast while all of our friends conquer the world." She laughed softly as she took a long drink of her coffee.

"Alright, well I'd sure like it if you two held it down together," I said lifting my eyebrows.

She rolled her eyes and shooed me away with her hand, but kept the smile on her face. "You just go wake up your pretty girlfriend. I'm doing just fine here in Andiland."

Laughing as I walked away, I found Scarlett just as I had suspected, sound asleep in the middle of her bed. Sliding my feet out of my shoes, I slipped under the covers next to her, and pulled her tiny frame next to me. "Hey, sleepyhead, it's time to get up," I whispered in her ear. She groaned and rolled away from me. I grabbed her hips and pulled her back to me. "Scarlett MacGregor, you better get your pretty little ass up. We have a flight to catch to our new home." Still refusing to open her eyes, she groaned and rolled away again. This time I climbed on top of her and was going to tickle her into waking up, but right before I did, her eyes flew open and she started cracking up laughing. Ugh! That little faker! Just for her little stunt I decided to tickle her anyways.

As she squirmed underneath me, trying to escape while laughing so hard that she couldn't breathe, Max banged on the wall and yelled out, "Would you two please wait until you get to California to do that? I'm tired of listening to y'all having sex!" We both froze and looked at each other. Her mouth made an "o" shape as if she was shocked, and then we both started dying laughing again. Once we calmed down and caught our breath, we both went out to eat some breakfast.

Andi was still sitting on the couch, sipping her coffee and eating her doughnut, so we joined her and waited for grouchy Max to come out of his room. Sure enough, less than five minutes later, he came trudging down the hallway in his pajama pants and with his eyes half open.

"Hiya, Meaniehead Max," Scarlett said, as he plopped on the couch between her and Andi.

He grumbled some sort of hello before Andi said, "Don't you mean Masturbating Max?" Both she and Scarlett burst out in laughter immediately, and I tried really hard not to join them, but I couldn't help it. That smart little mouth was one of the reasons we loved Andi so much.

Max just rolled his eyes and looked at her. "Get me some coffee, brat."

"Get your own damn coffee, old man. You aren't following the three F's, so I don't take orders from you," she retorted smugly.

"Dare I ask what the three F's are?" he asked hesitantly.

She gave him this over-the-top sweet smile and answered, "Feeding, Financing, and Fucking."

He literally growled at her, taking her coffee out of her hands. "You sleep in my apartment more than anywhere else, so I do finance you in a way." He then grabbed a doughnut from the coffee table and stuck it in her mouth. "There, I just fed you." In one sweeping motion, he threw her over his shoulder and marched to his bedroom with her. I heard him say, "When we come out of this bedroom, I fully expect you to get me a coffee, *brat*." Then the door clicked shut.

For the second time in less than an hour, Scarlett and I just looked at each other stunned. "Well, I'm kinda sad we aren't sticking around to see how this plays out," she finally murmured. I nodded as I finished off my coffee, "Yes, I have a feeling it's gonna get a little interesting."

I stood up to throw my cup away and she followed. "I just need to shower and get dressed and I'll be ready to go. Give me like forty five minutes." I kissed her forehead and swatted her ass as she retreated to the bathroom.

As promised, a little less than an hour later, Scarlett came out of her room, dressed in a long black sundress and sandals. I took one look at her and was reminded of why I was so ecstatic about this move. I was going to spend the rest of my life with her. "You look beautiful, butterfly. Are you ready to do this?"

She chewed her bottom lip nervously. "Yes, but I kinda wanted to tell them bye before we left," she said nodding her head towards Max's bedroom door.

"Max is taking us to the airport, silly. Remember, so that Andi can keep the car."

"Oh, right... sorry. I've just been so crazy making sure everything is ready for us when we get there, I completely forgot about the car and stuff."

"Just knock on the door and tell them we are about ready to leave."

Just a couple of minutes after she knocked, they both came out of his room, grinning like giddy adolescents.

"You crazy Californians ready for this?" he asked, his mood obviously improved.

"Yep, I just need to throw Scarlett's suitcase in the trunk, and we are good to go."

"Well, let's do this," he said, patting my back as he walked by me.

I honestly didn't think they had just had sex, Max had more respect for Andi than that, but I did think it was leading there soon. I did notice that Andi had grabbed the leftover cup of coffee, warmed it up in the microwave, and handed it to Max before we all walked out the door. It appeared it was a day for new beginnings for all of us.

SCARLETT

Thankfully Ash and I had shipped most of our stuff to his sister before we left, so all we had to take on the plane was one suitcase each with a couple changes of clothes and our toiletries. Our flight was direct from Houston to Oakland and from there we took a taxi to our new apartment. Crys and Will were there waiting for us with our boxes when we finally arrived early afternoon. They had both really been a godsend in helping coordinate the entire move. Even though they lived like four or five hours away, they had driven up the coast one weekend to apartment hunt for us. Pictures online could be very deceiving and we were also not familiar with the neighborhoods, so they had taken notes and pictures and sent them with their overall gut feelings on the different places. Once we chose a place and paid the deposit and rent, they spent another weekend furniture shopping. I didn't want to get to our new home and sleep in a sleeping bag our first night, so again they had made the trip to get our place furnished.

When the taxi dropped us off in the parking lot of the apartment complex, Ash and I kind of stood there a minute just looking at each other. The moment was almost surreal, after all of the months of planning, we were about to walk into our new home in California! Then a voice broke through our moment, "Ash! Scarlett! We are up here!" We pulled our gaze from each other and up to where his sister and brother-in-law stood waving on a second floor balcony.

"Let's go home, butterfly," he said as we both began walking in their direction.

I had seen many photos that Crys had sent of the surrounding area as well as the apartment itself, but it just seemed different seeing it through my own eyes... better. As soon as we walked through the door, we were both engulfed in hugs and kisses by Crys. She squealed about how excited she was and how she hoped everything was perfect. Will, with his usual laid back disposition, waited for us to get into the apartment before saying hello and how happy he was that we were going to be closer.

Finally, I had a chance to look around at the place. I was instantly in love. Crys had done an amazing job of decorating and getting everything set up. The living room was very contemporary, a lot of straight edges and a ton of color, and I dug the vibrancy of it. The kitchen was an extension of the living room. Many of the smaller appliances were candy apple red and she had decorated with a splash of animal prints; again, I was very pleased.

In addition to the living room and kitchen, the apartment had two bedrooms. I first peeked into the secondary bedroom that we had requested to be set up as an office-slash-studio. We both wanted a place where we could escape to do homework and to play music. The room had a very Japanese garden ambiance which I though was just perfect. Finally, I stepped into the master, and I was breathless. It was everything I could've ever imagined and more. The furniture all had a dark chocolate finish and she had chosen a palette of blues for the bedding and décor. The queen-sized, four poster bed in the middle of the room looked like something a Disney princess would sleep in. In addition to the fluffy pillows that covered the bed, a light blue organza had been draped around the top of the posters for a faux canopy appearance. The room was filled with an overall serene and tranquil ambiance; it was impeccable. The same aura of the master flowed over into the en suite bathroom. Blues and dark brown towels hung from the towel rack, and it made me feel like I was in a day spa.

As I eventually finished my solo tour, the three of them waited for me in the living room, their faces eagerly awaiting my verdict. I didn't say anything, I just picked Crys up and swung her around in a circle, kissing her cheek as I sat her down.

Ash was beaming. "I think that means she likes it, sis," he joked.

Crystal laughed. "I hope so. I think I like it better than my house. Will and I may just stay here and send you guys to our place to the munchkins."

"I love my nephews like crazy, but there's no way in hell I want to live those beasts. I wonder who their parents could be," he teased.

"Oh, shush your mouth, little brother. Soon enough that will be you, and I can't wait to remind you of your comments," she said with a smirk. She then turned her attention to me. Will and I did a little bit of grocery shopping for the basics, but of course you'll need to go get all of the stuff that you like. We just wanted you to have food to eat in case you didn't make it to the store for a few days."

"I really can't thank you enough for everything. The apartment, the décor, the groceries... everything; you've made this the easiest move across country in history. I'm so very grateful."

"Think nothing of it, I had a blast doing it," she replied with Will nodding in agreement next to her. "But I do know that you both probably want some time to get settled in. We were thinking that we could all grab a bite to eat so that you don't have to dirty up your kitchen, and then the two of us got a hotel room for the night instead of driving back. We plan to thoroughly enjoy a night without children." She grabbed Will's arm and gave him a silly, pervy wink.

Ash cut her off before she could say anything else. "Okay, that's enough of where that conversation was going. I think that's a fabulous idea, I'm starving. Let's get something quick so that Scarlett and I can get unpacked and check out the new place fully."

An hour later we were fed and saying final thank you's and goodbyes to the two of them as they dropped us off back at our new home. We already had plans to visit them for the July fourth weekend so we knew that it wouldn't be long before we saw each other again. Completely exhausted from the day's activities and the stress that had built up prior to the move, Ash and I both showered and passed out before nine o'clock that night. Wrapped securely in his arms, I got the best night of sleep of my entire life.

CHAPTER TWENTY
Where I Come From ~ Passion Pit
Awake My Soul ~ Mumford & Sons

MASON

Life in Austin was good. Ever since I had been back, things seemed to be moving along near perfectly. The guys and I picked up our friendship like I hadn't been gone and musically we seemed to be clicking like never before. We got back in the studio almost immediately and began working on the songs that I had written while away. It felt so good to be making music with my closest friends again; I knew without a doubt it was what I was supposed to be doing.

It took them a little while to adjust to the new and improved Rat, the one that didn't care about partying, getting drunk or high, or girls. Okay, that wasn't completely true. I still was very interested in females, the problem was the one female I truly wanted wasn't available to me. No matter how hard I tried to tell myself to move on, to leave the past in the past, she always seemed to find her way back in my thoughts and dreams. Even though we didn't see each other regularly any more, Scarlett and I still texted daily and even talked on the phone occasionally. I knew that the continued conversation made it even harder to let go, but I needed her friendship and support even more.

I did try to go out with a few girls that either Aaron's girlfriend, Sophie, set me up with or girls I met at the gym, but it always felt so forced. I had made the decision that I wasn't having anything to do with groupies or any girl that I met at one of our shows. If and when I did find someone, I wanted them to go out with me for me, not because I was the lead singer of a band. Another bit of good news I received when I returned was that Bentley had moved her bitch ass to Los Angeles. I was not looking forward to having to see her on a regular basis, so her being gone made things that much better.

About a month after getting resettled, Jobu's Rum began to play shows locally again. We were hoping that when Jag returned from the tour he was on with VanderBlue the following month that he would begin lining us up some bigger venues and possibly organizing a tour for us to open for. We wanted to get our new lineup perfected in addition to getting our name back out there, so we were playing any and every thing that came our way. Ever since

I had been sober, I had fallen in love with music all over again. It was almost like when I got my first guitar in middle school and I came home and practiced every single day. I just couldn't get enough to satisfy my hunger for it.

On Saturday of Memorial Day weekend, we were lined up to play at the Lucky Lounge, a pretty well-known live music venue, which was a really big deal for us especially on a holiday weekend that marked the beginning fofsummer. I was happy to have something to keep my mind busy as I knew that Scarlett was moving that weekend, and I really didn't need to dwell on that. The place was jam packed and the vibe in the air was intoxicating on its own. By the time we took the stage, I was definitely buzzing on adrenaline, and evidently the rest of the guys were too, because we were all spot on. The music from the different instruments bled together in perfect harmony and I was singing from the depths of my soul. We ended our set with Passenger's *Let Her Go*, the same song I had sang to Scarlett that night at Empty's, and the crowd's reaction when we finished was so powerful that it gave me goose bumps from head to toe.

After the show, all the guys were heading up to the bar for a celebratory drink, and as tempted as I was, I told them I was calling it a night and heading back to the apartment. As I was making my way through the club to the door, arms circled my waist from behind. I turned around to tell whoever it was that I wasn't interested in any company, but was pleasantly surprised to look down into those stunning blue eyes that I had become familiar with.

"Kiddo! What are you doing here?" I asked as I picked her up, hugging her tightly and kissing her cheek.

Andi giggled as she wrapped her arms around my neck, squeezing back. "We came to see you sing, silly."

I looked around to see who was with her. "We?" That was when I saw Max standing back a little, waiting while she and I said our hellos. Still holding her, I walked over to him and gave him a man hug. "Max, dude, thank you so much for coming. That's fucking awesome. I'm shocked," I said to him.

He smiled warmly and replied, "Of course, the show was amazing. Y'all have come a long way from Empty's, I'm really impressed."

"Thanks, I appreciate it."

Andi tapped at the ring in my lip. "What is this?" Then she ran her palm over my freshly buzzed hair. "And where did all of your hair go?" Finally, she slapped my chest. "And why didn't you tell me you were a big rock star? I was living with a famous person!"

Laughing hard, I slid her down my body to put her back on the ground. "Aren't you just full of questions," I teased her.

She looked up at me with her sassy look. "Well, I made Max drive here so that I can see you, and you look all different and I find out you're kind of a big deal. I'm just a little shocked."

I shook my head at her. "I'm just Mase with no hair and my lip ring back in, kiddo. And I'm no big deal, but I wouldn't mind being one someday." Turning my attention to Max, I asked him, "Where are you guys staying tonight? If I'd have known you were coming, y'all could've stayed with me."

"Nah, that's okay. She wanted to surprise you, so we just got a hotel room. We are gonna stay until Monday... ya know, we're just gonna do a little sightseeing cause she's never been to Austin before." She slid up next to his side, and he put his arm around her shoulder as he kissed her temple. "This was a last minute trip. After we dropped them off at the airport this morning, we decided to look online to see if we could find out where y'all were playing... so here we are."

I knew exactly who he was referring to with *them*, and I appreciated him not saying their names. I also was very curious about what was going on between Max and Andi. I assumed if anything had happened Scarlett would've told me, but all she had said was that Andi spent a lot of time with them and that they had become really close. Pushing away my mental commentary, I told them both. "Well I was just headed to grab a bite to eat before going home. Would y'all like to join me?"

They looked at each other, speaking silently, and then she said, "Actually, we're both pretty tired from driving and everything, but do you have time to meet us tomorrow afternoon before your next show?"

"Absolutely, kiddo. How's two o'clock for a late lunch?"

"Perfect." She stepped towards me to hug me bye, and even with her on her tiptoes, I had to squat down to kiss the top of her head. I shook Max's hand and told them both that I'd see them the next afternoon before heading out to my bike.

As I laid in bed a little while later, I couldn't help but think how strange things seemed. Scarlett and Ash were in California, Andi and Max were in a hotel room together in Austin, and I was alone on a Saturday night after a show. Just about that time, my phone began vibrating on the nightstand. I looked at the clock and saw that it was nearly four o'clock in the morning. Who in the hell? I reached across the bed and saw that it was Jag.

"Hello," I answered.

"Rat, sorry if I woke you up, but I wanted to call you immediately," he said excitedly.

"Dude, where are you and what time is it there?"

He chuckled, "I'm in London and it's almost ten here. We've got two shows left this weekend and then we are heading home. Thank God, I'm so tired of living out of a suitcase."

I really didn't feel bad for him at all. I was supposed to be on that tour, but I had gone and fucked it up. "So what's up? This better be good for a call at this hour."

"What? Were you asleep? I figured after your big show tonight, you'd be out celebrating."

"Sleeping *is* celebrating for me now, and how did you know about the show?"

"That's why I'm calling," he began to explain. "I don't know what y'all did tonight, but I got a call from an exec at a top tier label company who saw you and he was blown out of the water. He wants to meet with us next week about signing on, and he's already talking about a late summer tour."

I was speechless. All I could muster up was a "wow."

Jag laughed hard on the other end of the line. "No kidding! Look, go back to sleep, old man; we'll talk about it more when I get back on Tuesday, but let the guys know, and strap your seat belt on cause it looks like we're about to go for a ride."

I hung up the phone and just stared at it. That was the phone call I had been waiting for most of my life. It was finally happening.

SCARLETT

The first month or so in California was everything I had thought they would be. Ash didn't start work until the first of July so we had the entire month of June to spend together, hanging out and discovering northern California. I absolutely fell in love with the scenery and culture that surrounded us, and I enjoyed exploring the Pacific coast with him as he found new surf spots to try out. Several days each week, we would pack up a blanket, a picnic lunch, and his boards and just take off down Highway One. We would stop at small little beaches and he would surf for several hours as I sunbathed and read on the blanket. The climate was surprisingly cooler than I had expected, but it was nice to lay out for a while and not be covered in sweat.

In addition, I got caught up on all of my reading that I had neglected during finals. There were days that I really wished Evie had been there so that I could discuss my undying love for Lucien Knight, my hatred for girls named Bekah and Nan, and my secret desire to have Remington Tate's babies, but instead I wrote down my thoughts about the books in letters to her. One day when I was at the beach, I had forgotten my journal, where I typically wrote the letters, so I typed up my letter on my iPad instead. That was when I got the idea to start a blog for the letters.

That night I did all kinds of research about different blogging sites and taught myself about widgets, hyperlinks, favicons, and a ton of other different blogging terms. The following day I spent setting up the blog. I titled it *Ever Afters for Evie* and began entering all of the letters that I had already written. I could've cared less if anyone else ever read it; for me, it was how I could stay connected to my best friend that I missed dearly. It was my way of keeping her caught up on all of the books she was missing.

That evening Ash came up behind me as I sat madly entering posts on my laptop. "Hey, butterfly, whatcha been doing all day? You've hardly come up for air."

I stopped typing and smiled at him over my shoulder. "I set up a blog today! Do you want to see it?"

He nodded and sat down on the couch next to me. "It's a place where I'm doing book reviews for Evie, so that I can tell her all of the things I would've told her if she was here," I explained excitedly. "I'm really loving it! Right now, I'm entering all of the handwritten letters I had already done."

He grabbed my journal and flipped it over in his hand. "I wondered what in the world you were writing in here all of the time, but I didn't want to be nosy and ask."

I laughed softly and leaned over to kiss his cheek. "Well, now you know. And if you want, you can follow my amaze-balls blog too," I teased.

He cupped my face in his hands and kissed me firmly on the lips. "Please understand if I don't want to read about you swooning over fictional characters, but I am happy that you found something that makes you happy. You need a release, and I know that it's hard here since you haven't made any friends yet. That will all change once school starts."

I nodded and swallowed hard. He was right. As happy as I was with him in our new place, I was pretty lonely. I texted and Skyped with Andi and Mina pretty much every day. I stayed current on the Andi/ Max relationship, which was moving slower than molasses.

I just wanted to thump that boy on the head sometimes, but I knew that he had to be okay with moving on in his head... if he forced it before he was ready, it wouldn't have a chance of lasting. I also texted with Mase a couple of times a week, but he was so busy that I knew it was hard for him to find time. He and Jobu's Rum had signed with some big label and they were in the studio like non-stop recording their first album before they went on tour. He was supposed to send me the tour dates and cities as soon as he found out in hopes that we'd be able to see one of his shows close to us. I was really happy for him and the success that was headed his way. He had been clean for over six months and his entire attitude had changed. I was extremely proud of his transition, and at times I really missed his contagious smile.

Almost as if he knew I had been thinking about him, later that night I got a text that gave me something else to look forward to.

MASE: July 31st opening show at Hard Rock Las Vegas. I'd love if y'all could make it.

I had never been to Vegas before, and I really wanted to see his very first show on the tour... now I just had to convince Ash to go.

CHAPTER TWENTY ONE
Seabreeze ~ Tyrone Wells
I Can't Stop ~ Flux Pavilion

ASH

"Ash, wake up! It's time for breakfast," Scarlett's voice carried into our bedroom from the kitchen.

"I'll be there in just a minute!" I called back, savoring every last minute I had in bed. It was my first day of work at the Lawrence Berkeley National Laboratory, and even though I was extremely excited about beginning the next phase of my life, I was also sad that I wouldn't be spending the days with Scarlett any longer. The past six weeks we had spent together had been nothing short of amazing. Sightseeing, days at the beach, trying new restaurants... all of it had been incredible, but the time for fun had to come to an end and it was time to be a grown up.

I slowly climbed out of bed and made my way into the kitchen where I found her pouring a glass of milk. She skipped over to greet me, kissing me on the cheek. "Morning, sunshine. Your breakfast and coffee are ready. Did you sleep well?" I grumbled a "mornin" and sat down at the breakfast bar where she had our plates waiting.

She laughed softly as she sat down next to me. "I thought you'd be excited about today. Haven't you been looking forward to this?" She picked up a piece of bacon from my plate and brought it to my mouth. I parted my lips, allowing her to feed me, and grunted at her question. She frowned and took a bite herself.

"I've just had such a good time hanging out with you, I'm going to miss you during the days. I don't want to leave you here by yourself," I whined.

"Awww... that's so sweet of you. I've had a great summer too... all of our day trips, hanging out with your sister and Will, all of it, but I don't want you to not enjoy your first day cause you're worried about me being lonely. I'm gonna do my usual ~ read, blog, play some music... I'll keep myself busy, love."

"I know, it's just a little bittersweet, ya know," I said as I devoured the plate of food in front of me.

She nodded. "Yeah, I understand, but I want you to go lose yourself in all those particles and gamma rays and whatever the hell else you'll be working with."

I got up to put my dishes in the sink, kissing the top of her head on the way by. "I'll be good, butterfly. I'm gonna shower and get ready now."

Thirty minutes later I was headed down the highway on my way in to my first day on the job. As soon as I parked and checked in through security, I was greeted by a guy named Louis who was my trainer. The first thing he did was walk me around the massive institute, pointing out things and places that I would need to know. We then made the way to the office that he and I shared, where he jumped right in showing me the project he was working on. Enthralled by the complexity of the work and the overall massiveness of the facility, I got right to work with him. Louis turned out to be a pretty cool guy, and I was thankful that I was paired with someone so easy to get along with. Before I knew it, lunchtime was upon us, and what seemed not long after that, it was time to go home.

Scarlett had dinner nearly ready when I got home that evening. As soon as I came through the door, I picked her up and kissed her hard. "Hi, butterfly, how was your day? It smells delicious in here, by the way."

She mumbled against my lips, "My day was good. I did everything I told you I was gonna do, plus cooked you dinner." Tapping the end of my nose with her finger, she continued, "But don't get used to this. I'm not turning into Martha Stewart... I just wanted to celebrate your first day... which I'm dying to hear about."

I sat her back down on the ground. "Okay, just let me change into comfy clothes real quick and then I'll tell you all about it."

We spend the next hour enjoying her homemade lasagna and just talking about our days. Then she dropped the question on me. "I need to talk to you about something," she began nervously. "As I've told you, Jobu's Rum is going on tour later this year, and well... Mase texted me that their first show is gonna be in Vegas on July thirty first, and he wants us to come."

I snorted. "I'm sure he wants *us* to come."

She sighed at my response. "Well that's what his text said. I thought it would be nice to support him at his first big show, plus I'd like to see Vegas."

I wasn't thrilled with the idea, but I could definitely do with a Vegas trip, I asked, "What day of the week is it on?"

"Thursday."

"Scarlett, there's no way that I can take off work for that. I just started today, there's I can't ask off already... especially with us having a deadline coming up," I explained.

Groaning, she sat back in her chair, looking at me with her sad puppy dog eyes, but saying nothing. I hated seeing her disappointed and sad, but I knew it was literally impossible for me to take any time. Then I did the unthinkable ~ I asked her if she wanted to go by herself. Holy shit! I needed my brain checked. As soon as the words were out of my mouth, I wanted to take them back.

"Are you serious right now?" Her face lit up like a Christmas tree, looking at me in disbelief.

"Well I'm not sure how much fun Vegas will be since you aren't twenty one, but if you want to go to the show, there's no reason you can't fly down there that day and come home the next. I trust you and I know that it's important to you."

She flew out of her chair and into my lap, hugging and kissing me. "Oh, thank you! Thank you!"

I held her tight and kissed her back, hoping I wasn't making a mistake.

~   ~   ~   ~   ~

Three weeks came and went in what seemed like three days. I was living the life I had always dreamed of. The work I was doing was just bad ass, there was no other way of putting it. I knew that I had made the right decision in not only my career field but the place I had chosen to work at. I was closer with my sister than I had been in years, and even though I didn't live close to my mom anymore, we talked frequently and I knew that she was finally happy with her life. And then there was Scarlett... my butterfly... my Psyche. She wasn't perfect, but she was perfect for me, and that's all I needed. I was overjoyed that she had taken to the move so well. She had really delved into her new blog and her music, and watching her blissfully float around the apartment, made me feel like a king.

The day that she left for Vegas, I was a bit nervous about her traveling alone, but I reminded myself that she was plenty capable of getting where to she needed to go. I never thought I'd think it, but I felt comfortable knowing that she'd be with Mason when she was there. Crazy, I know, but I was confident that he would keep her safe and not allow anything to happen. I couldn't live the rest of my life scared something was going to happen between them. I knew that they were special to each other, and would always have a love and respect for one another, but for whatever reason, she had chosen to be with me.

I dropped her off at the airport on my way to work that morning, kissing her long and hard on her full lips. "Remember... have fun. Don't get arrested or married while you're there," I joked.

She rolled her eyes and laughed at me. "I'll try not to."

Embracing her one last time, I whispered in her ear, "I love you, butterfly... 'your curves and all your edges, and all your perfect imperfections.' I'll see you tomorrow night."

"I love you, too, Ash. 'You're my end and my beginning; even when I lose, I'm winning,'" she whispered back. Then she grabbed her bag and headed for the security check point. Right before turning the corner where I couldn't see her anymore, she looked back at me and blew me a kiss and made hand hearts. Damn, she was beautiful. I stood there for several minutes with a goofy ass grin on my face. I wasn't expecting her to sing the next lyrics of the song to me, but it filled me with an indescribable feeling of warmth and love.

That afternoon at work, Louis and I actually hit a part in the project where we couldn't move any further until we received info from a different team, and surprisingly, we were excused early. When I got to the apartment, the quiet and emptiness of it began to eat at me almost immediately, so I decided to change clothes and throw my board in the car for a late afternoon session. There was nothing else in the world that I had experienced that could compare to the feeling of surfing. Being out in the middle of the expansive ocean, the smell of the seabreeze, the sound of the waves crashing onto the shore, the exhilarating feeling of riding an incredible force of nature... it was my heaven on earth.

Paddling out into the endless blue waters, the endorphins began to pump through my body, inspired and exhilarated. I made it out to the first break with relative ease, and sat up on my board waiting for the next set to come in. There weren't very many people out that afternoon which was a welcome sight. I hated competing with a bunch of people for a wave. As I saw the swell begin to form behind me, I laid down on my belly and begin to paddle into the first wave. I hopped up on the board, just as I had done a thousand times, but somehow the leash wrapped around my ankle awkwardly and snapped. I never caught my balance and purged forward off the front of the board. I tried to surface, but for some reason I kept getting pulled under. Spinning underneath the water in an undertow, I lost my sense of direction and couldn't tell which way was up and which way was down. I tried telling myself not to panic, but my body instinctively fought the current. Finally, I just let go, relaxing my body and thinking about Scarlett's beautiful face that I would see the next day.

SCARLETT

Getting off of the plane in Las Vegas was a bit overwhelming. I wasn't sure what I was expecting, but slot machines in the terminal, definitely wasn't it. I had never traveled anywhere alone before and I was a little nervous at first, but the enthusiasm began to take over quickly. As I walked through the airport, the buzz of the people combined with the constant dinging from the multitude of machines got my adrenaline pumping. Since I was only staying one night, I had fit all of my clothes and stuff into a carry on, so I bypassed baggage claim and went straight out to the taxi line.

Fifteen minutes later, I was dropped off outside of the Hard Rock Hotel and Casino and I hesitantly ventured inside. Once I stepped through the front doors, I was completely mesmerized. Thankfully one of the employees found me standing with my mouth gaping open in the foyer and helped me find the line to check in my room. Upon giving my name to the lady behind the counter, she smiled brightly at me and said, "Welcome, Miss MacGregor. I see that you'll be staying in the Stones Suite for your stay here. I have you just down for this one night. Is that correct?"

Confused, I pulled out my reservation from my purse. "Well, yes I'm just here for tonight, but I didn't book any suite. I just had a regular room."

She looked at her computer screen, reading through something, then looked back up at me. "It appears that you've been upgraded as a guest of Jobu's Rum, and you are indeed staying in the Stones Suite, ma'am."

A few minutes later, she gave me a little folder with my room keys in it and reminded me that check out was noon the following day. I thanked her several times, still in shock over the upgrade, and followed her directions to the correct elevator bank. I only had to stop and ask directions once as I traveled through the half mile maze to get to the all-suite tower. Finally, I made it to my room. I slid the key card into the device and upon activation of the green light, I stepped into the most luxurious room I had ever seen in my life.

The living room area of the suite was decorated in gray, white, and a muted purple, and combined with the soft lighting and ceiling adorned in crystals, it truly felt like I was inside an amethyst. I continued further into the room, through a doorway, which led me to the bedroom. I think my heart stopped beating when I saw not only the huge four-poster, king-sized bed in the middle of the room, but the huge flower arrangement of every shade of pink flower that existed sitting on the banquet at the end of the bed. In addition, there was a basket of wine and chocolates on the bed and a box gift wrapped in silver paper with a huge pink bow on top of it. I slowly made my way over to the bed, noting that the box did indeed have my name scrawled across the small card. I dropped my bag to the floor and opened the card to read the note.

> *Scarlett,*
>
> *I can't thank you enough for being here for me... not just tonight but always. Because of you, I have come to realize that I do deserve to be loved, and most importantly, I've learned to love myself. I'm not there yet, but I'm much closer than I've ever been to finding my euphoria. Here's a little something to remind you to never stop until you get there too. Later I'll show you my new reminder*
>
> *I'll see you tonight after the show, Angel.*
>
> > *Love you always,*
> >
> > *Mase*

With trembling hands, I opened the package, anxious to see what was inside but scared at the same time. I opened the top of the Pandora box and found a beautiful charm bracelet staring back at me. When I took the bracelet out of the box to better study it, I saw that each charm was separated with a diamond encrusted pink spacer. However there was no holding back the tears as I ran my fingers over each of the five charms: a guitar, a piano, a heart, an open book that had "Ever Afters for Evie" engraved on it, and finally, angel wings with the word Euphoria etched on the back. It absolute perfection. I had no other words.

An hour or so later, I changed into my solid black bikini and decided to go down to the pool for a couple hours of sunbathing before meeting Aaron's girlfriend, Sophie, and Smiley for dinner. Before I left my room, I sent Ash a quick text letting him know that I had made it safely.

ME: Hey babe, just letting you know that I made it safe and sound. Heading down to the pool and then dinner with the girls before the show. I hope your day at work is good. See you tomorrow night. I love you! ~ Butterfly

Not that I should've been surprised at that point, but the pool area was just as breathtaking as the rest of the resort. Because I was staying in one of the suites, I got a complimentary cabana at the Paradise beach area. When I gave the waitress my name and room number, she told me that all of my food and drinks had been taken care of; I was to simply relax and enjoy. I ordered one of their specialty drinks, thankful that she didn't ask for any identification, and did just as she said. I laid back with my ear buds in, ereader on my lap, and frozen yumminess in my hand and dove into the second installment of Jake Wethers, which I felt was completely appropriate seeing that I was going to a rock concert that night.

Just after seven o'clock that night, I was putting the final touches on my makeup when there was a knock at the door. I looked down to make sure that my robe was covering me completely and went to see who was there. I thought I couldn't be surprised any more that day, but when I opened the door, Max and Andi were standing there with huge smiles on their faces and dressed for a night on the town. Squealing commenced followed by a bunch of jumping around and hugging.

"What in the world are y'all doing here?" I shrieked once we had all calmed down a bit.

"Oh, I don't know... we just decided to fly to Vegas for the hell of it," Max said sarcastically.

I rolled my eyes at him. "Well, come in, come in. I'm almost finished getting ready. Please make yourselves at home. I'm supposed to be meeting Sophie and Smiley for dinner in about twenty minutes at the steakhouse downstairs."

They both walked into the suite, looking around, obviously as impressed as I was. "Wow, this room is amazing," Andi said. "And yes, we know, we are going to dinner too. No one told you so that we would be a surprise."

My face was starting to hurt I was smiling so much. I just couldn't believe how amazing the day had been. "Okay, well let me finish getting dressed real quick. I shouldn't be any more than ten minutes. Y'all take a look at the bedroom too, it's so posh; I feel like a rock star myself here."

In the bathroom, I quickly changed into my a short black dress and black heels. I looked at my reflection in the mirror, pleased with what I saw. The dress was sexy but not slutty, and as if all the stars were aligned just perfectly, my hair and makeup looked pretty good too. Evie would've been so proud.

Stepping back into the bedroom, I burst out laughing as Max and Andi were sitting on the bed, helping themselves to a glass of wine and some of the chocolates from the basket. Max looked up at me, with a smirk. "You said make yourself at home." Both of them started giggling like little kids and I couldn't help but think how cute they were together.

"Come on you two, you're going to ruin your dinner," I scolded them as I shooed them off of the bed. "Let's go downstairs."

Right before we walked out the door, I grabbed my new charm bracelet off of the night stand and clasped it around my wrist. I looked down at it, thinking what a perfect day this had turned out to be. I only wish that Ash could've been there too.

CHAPTER TWENTY TWO
Counting Stars ~ One Republic
Chemistry of a Car Crash ~ Shiny Toy Guns

MASON

I was a nervous fucking wreck. Damn if I didn't crave a shot or five of whiskey for the first time in over seven months. I had been on stage in front of people hundreds, maybe thousands, of times before, but for some reason, that night seemed so different... so significant. Jobu's Rum had finally gotten our big break ~ we were headlining in Las Vegas to kick off our tour! It was if the night set the tone for the next four months of shows, and I wanted it to be flawless.

My schedule had been booked solid from nine o'clock that morning straight through until show time. After breakfast, we had interviews, followed by a photo shoot, and then a sound check. We were fed a late-lunch-slash-early-dinner before attending an autograph signing and photo hour. There was barely enough time to shower and get dressed before we were due backstage for the show. Everything was so different from when we opened for VanderBlue, when we just showed up, went on stage to perform, and then hung out backstage signing a few autographs. We were really given the star treatment, and it was cool as shit. I made sure to tell Jag how appreciative I was several times throughout the day.

As I got dressed for the show, I wondered how Scarlett's day had gone. I had done everything I could possibly think of to make it a day that she'd remember forever too. She had played such a huge role in getting me to that point, and I wanted to not just show my gratitude, but to let her know that I would always love her and wanted the best for her always. I stood in front of the mirror in just my jeans and ran my fingers over the word I had tattooed on my upper chest. Euphoria. It was my reminder every day of what I was striving for. I smiled as I thought about her reaction when she opened the bracelet. I really hoped she loved it; I thought long and hard about each of those charms and I knew each one would be special to her. Flying Max and Andi out to be with her once I found out she was coming alone was just a bonus. I loved knowing that the three of them, along with Marcus, would be in the front row, experiencing it first hand with me.

Cruz tapped on the door and walked in the bathroom without waiting for a response. "You ready for this, man?" he asked me.

I turned away from the mirror and looked at him. "More ready than I've ever been. Let's do this." I slid the plain, fitted black t-shirt over my head and my feet in my black and white checkered chucks before following him out of the room.

The closer we got to show time, the more relaxed I got surprisingly enough. There were a ton of people backstage; I didn't have any idea who half of them were. I practiced some of the stress relieving techniques that Heather had taught me, and got myself into a happy, secure place mentally. Jag came into the waiting room and told us it was time to follow him out. When we took the stage, the cheers from the crowd were overwhelming. I looked out into the audience and all I could see was a sea of people. Our first single, *She'll Never Know,* from the new album had released two weeks prior and had done well on the charts, but I had no idea that many people even knew we existed.

Before we began our first song, I thanked everyone for coming out and being a part of such an epic night for Jobu's Rum, especially our family and friends that had made the trip to see us. I looked down at all of them when I made the comment, overjoyed to see each of their faces. Then, wasting no more time, we began what would end up being the best show of my life. The excitement buzzing through the air was electric, and every one of us felt it deep in our bones. The music flowed out of us like it was what we were born to do. At one point, I ripped my shirt off and gave it to Scarlett. I was like a man possessed; the music had completely taken over my body. We played through many of the songs on our latest album as well as a couple that would come out on the next one. As the show was nearing the end, the lights were brought down a little and I took a moment to address the crowd again.

"I just wanted to thank you all again for coming out this evening. We've got two more songs for you before we wrap it up, and I just wanted to say something about them beforehand. This next song we are going to play is a cover of one of my favorite songs. I first played it one night in my brother's bar back in Houston by myself, and at that time it summed up how I was feeling about someone spot on. Then, once the band started playing together again, it was how we ended each of our shows. The last song, which is our latest single, is actually the song I wrote in response to the first one. I think it'll all make sense here in a minute." I winked at the crowd, which was answered by a deafening roar of screams and whistles.

I grabbed the stool sitting on the side of the stage and we played our version of Let Her Go once again. However, at the end of the song, Sebastian played a bass line that led us straight into the next. During that time, I looked down at Scarlett and said, "I hope you always know." Then I poured my heart out into the last song of the night.

Dark and dirty I couldn't find my way out
Shiny and white you never had any doubt
Together a mess that could only be made in Heaven

So can you tell me where my Heaven went
Who's bright idea was it to let her go
Can you tell me where my Heaven went
My biggest fear is that she'll never know

Lost and confused it was you that I feared
Eager and ready you allowed me to steer
Together a mess that could only be made in Heaven

So can you tell me where my Heaven went
Who's bright idea was it to let her go
Can you tell me where my Heaven went
My biggest fear is that she'll never know

An angel and a devil that fell in love
Chaos created and it fit like a glove
Together a mess that could only be created in Heaven

So can you tell me where my Heaven went
Who's bright idea was it to let her go
Can you tell me where my Heaven went
My biggest fear is that she'll never know

My biggest fear is that she'll never know
She'll never know that I loved her so

A thunderous roar of applause accompanied by a standing ovation followed the last note of the song. We took our bows and ran off the stage straight into our dressing room. I felt higher in that moment than I ever had on any drug; it was out of this world. We took a few minutes alone as a band, to both calm down and exchange some serious man-love. Then we opened the door to frenzy of people waiting for us. I cut through the crowd of mostly females pawing and pulling at me, looking for one person. As soon as my eyes found her, I could feel my heart beat again and I remembered to breathe.

I ran up to her and scooped her in my arms, hugging her so tightly I may have bruised her ribs. I could feel her crying on my shoulder, and I only prayed they were happy tears. I sat her back on her feet and looked in her eyes, "Why are you crying, Angel?"

She smiled through her tears, "I'm just so proud of you. You were fucking amaze-balls, Hotpants."

I threw my head back, laughing, "Did you just say *fucking* and *balls*, both in the same sentence? And call me Hotpants?"

She giggled and nodded hard. "I think I did. All of this debauchery in Sin City must be wearing off on me," she joked.

Shaking my head, I put my arm around her shoulders and looked around for the rest of the gang. Standing off about ten feet were Marcus, Max, and Andi. I ran over and hugged each one of them, thanking them again for coming. Then I told all of them to follow me back to the room where they were having the after-party.

A few hours later, I was completely wiped out and all I wanted was to go to sleep. I looked around for the rest of the band and my friends and family and said good night to each of them. The party was still in full swing with the alcohol flowing and bodies grinding against each other in the middle of the dance floor, but I had no reservations at all about retreating to my room to get some much needed rest. As I was making my way to the door, I saw Scarlett standing and talking to one of the producers. I didn't much care if it was rude or not, I grabbed her hand and asked if I could talk to her for a minute. She politely excused herself from the guy and followed me out of the room.

"I just wanted to thank you again for being here. I know I've said it a gazillion times, but it really means a lot. I've missed you." I looked down at her wrist and saw the charm bracelet. I grinned and looked back up at her. "Did you like it?"

"Are you kidding? It's one of the best things I've ever been given; I know you put so much thought into it." She pushed up on her tiptoes and kissed me on the cheek. "Thank you for not just the bracelet, but for all of today. It's been an amazing experience."

"I'm actually headed to my room, I'm exhausted. Are you gonna stay down here a while longer?" I asked.

"Nah, I'm pretty tired too. I'll head that way as well. It's already after two and my plane leaves at eleven in the morning."

"I'll walk you to your room to make sure you get there safely," I said without giving her an option. I put my hand on the small of her back and walked us towards the elevators.

Once we made it to her door, I did my best not to get emotional, but damn if it wasn't hard. I knew that we'd still text and stuff, but since I was going to be on the road for the next several months, I didn't know when I'd see her again. I circled my arms around her waist and pulled her close to me. She wrapped her arms around my neck and held me just as tight. We stayed like that for several minutes before pulling away.

"Goodnight, Angel. Let me know that you made it home tomorrow," I said before turning around and heading back to the elevator.

"Mase," she called out. I turned around, half hoping she's ask me to stay but half hoping she wouldn't ask me to make that decision. My eyes caught hers, and she smiled so brightly that the hall lit up. "Never worry that I don't know; I've always known." She then slid her key card and disappeared behind the door.

SCARLETT

Once I slipped into my room, I immediately kicked my shoes off and stripped out of my dress. I didn't even bother putting my pajamas on; I just climbed into the lush bed in my panties, collapsing face first into the feathery softness. As I slid my arm under the pillow, one of the charms on the bracelet caught on the sheet, reminding me that I need to take it off. I unhooked the clasp and reached across the bed to lay it on the nightstand. It was then that I noticed the seventeen missed calls and texts on my phone.

Snatching it up quickly, I scrolled through it noting that the first few calls were from a number that I didn't recognize, but all of the subsequent calls and texts were from Crys. I listened to the first message and my heart stopped beating. I didn't even bother listening to the rest; I immediately called Crys back, I didn't care what time it was.

"Scarlett, oh thank God," she answered the phone. I could instantly tell she had been crying.

"What's wrong, Crys? What happened? Where's Ash" I asked frantically.

"I need you to come home as soon as possible, Scarlett. You're in Vegas, right?"

"Yes, I came for Jobu's Rum opening show. Why? What happened? Where is Ash?" I asked again, my voice getting more demanding.

"I'll explain everything when you get here. I've already looked at flights for you and the earliest one out of there is at six fifteen," she paused for a minute and I could hear her talking to people in the background but the sound was muffled. "So that's just in a few hours from now. When you get back, go to your apartment and we'll meet you there."

"No!" I screamed. "Tell me right now what is going on! You can't just leave me like this for the next few hours. Obviously something has happened to Ash, and damn it, I deserve to know what I'm coming home to!" My entire body was shaking with fear. I knew if she wasn't telling me, it must be bad. Mentally, I had already started preparing for the worst. Maybe he had a bad car crash and broke some bones or had a head injury...

"Scarlett, I don't want to do this over the phone. Try to calm down and I will see you in a few hours," she said calmly.

"Tell. Me. Now." I demanded through gritted teeth.

She let out a long sigh and then I heard her start crying. "He's gone, Scarlett. He's gone," she choked out through muffled sobs.

I hung up the phone on her and went completely numb.

CHAPTER TWENTY THREE
Slipped Away ~ Avril Lavigne

SCARLETT

I don't know how long I sat there; it could've been two minutes or two hours. Eventually I pulled myself off of the bed and put on some shorts and a t-shirt. I needed to call someone, but I wasn't sure who. I stared at my phone thinking that she was going to call back and tell me it was some sick joke, but that never happened. I looked at the clock for the hundredth time, but the numbers displayed had no meaning to me. I didn't know what I was doing.

I decided to call Max to let him know; he would want to know. He answered the phone cheerily, "Sweetheart! Where are you at? You disappeared from the party!" There was a ton of hooting and hollering in the background so I assumed that he was still downstairs.

"Umm yeah, I just wanted to let you know that I'm heading home," I said in a voice that didn't even sound like mine.

"Heading home? Scarlett, it's like four o'clock in the morning. Are you drunk?"

"No... not drunk, and yes, my flight is at six fifteen so I'm heading to the airport now."

"Hold on," he replied. I heard him excusing himself as he got out of the crowd. "Okay, sorry about that. What's going on? Did something happen with Mase?"

"No, nothing with Mase," I swallowed hard as I felt the tears pricking at my eyes. "I just need to go home."

"Scarlett, tell me what the fuck is going on!"

"Ash is dead," I blurted out.

"I'll be right there," was all I heard before he hung up.

It wasn't five minutes later, Max was beating on the door yelling at me to open it. I swung the door open to him and Andi, who both pulled me in their arms simultaneously. They were crying asking a bunch of questions. "What happened? When? Who called you? "Why did you just find out?"

I stood there like a rag doll, allowing their arms to hold me up. They walked me to the sofa where all three of us sat down. I didn't know the answers to any of their questions; I didn't ask Crys anything. What did it really matter how or when it happened? The only thing that mattered was that he was gone. I was never going to see his smile again, never going to hear his voice, never going to feel his lips on mine... I heard Max and Andi talking to each other but I wasn't processing what they were saying. It sounded like they were a million miles away.

The next thing I knew they had my bag and we were leaving the room. We stopped by their suite, where again I just sat in a trance on the couch. They were shuffling around hurriedly and speaking lowly to each other, and before I knew it we were out the door again. Then there was a taxi ride and the airport. They tried to get me to eat, but I just couldn't. I couldn't do anything. I knew that I should be thinking about something, but my brain just refused to work.

A couple of hours later the three of us were getting off of the plane in Oakland and yet back in another taxi. I remember giving the driver my address; I was somehow able to do that. When we got to the apartment, Robin, Crys, and Will were all there waiting. Max introduced himself and Andi, and then explained that they were in Vegas with me and were also good friends of Ash. I just sat down and stared into space.

Crys joined me on the couch and put her arm around me, pulling me in a tight hug. She didn't say anything, she just held me. Finally, I was able to muster up some words. "What happened?" I whispered into her chest.

"He was surfing; that's all we know. Another surfer found him washed up and called 911, but we was already gone by the time they got there," she explained softly as she rocked me back and forth in her arms. "They broke in his car and got his wallet and cell phone; that's how they identified him and got a hold of us."

"Surfing, wow. The thing that brought him the most joy is what killed him..." I murmured, closing my eyes.

I think I fell asleep in her arms, that or I fainted, but either way I woke up a while later in my bed. I slowly opened my eyes and laid there staring at his side of the bed, where he would never lay with me again. I ran my hand back and forth over the spot where he would've been, and that's when the tears began. The tears and the memories and thoughts, an emotional overload all at once, came flooding in. And I tried hard... damn, I tried so hard to push it away, but I couldn't. I cried and cried and cried. I cried until I passed out again from sheer exhaustion of crying.

The next time I woke up, Robin was sitting in the bed next to me, rubbing my back. Her tear stained cheeks broke my heart. It reminded me of Evie's parents and I remembered thinking then that no parent should have to bury their child. I looked up at her through my swollen eyes and she gave me a half-hearted smile.

"I know that you are scared that I don't like you very much, but I just wanted you to know that isn't the case. I understood why you left on Christmas and I understand why you were in Vegas. I know that you made my boy happy, and that's all I ever wanted. So please don't ever think that I don't like you or that this happened because you weren't here."

I sat up and crawled into her lap, looping my arms around her neck and laying my head on her shoulder. "I'm so sorry. I'm so very sorry," I cried softly.

She hugged me tightly. "There's no reason for you to be sorry, Scarlett. We're all devastated over this. I know that it hasn't sunk in for any of us completely yet, but the only way we will make it through this is together."

"I'm just so so sorry," I said again.

She stroked my hair. "Shh shh, that's enough of that. Now listen, I don't want to draw this all out with a funeral and all of that. None of us need to rehash this tragedy over and over again. Ash's dad is flying out here this evening. We are going to have his body cremated and tomorrow we are going to take the ashes out to the ocean. Whoever wants to say something can, and otherwise, we are going to return him to where he loved to be." She paused to kiss the top of my head. "I know this is so much all at once, but in the next couple of weeks you're going to have to decide if you want to stay here and go to school like you planned or if you want to go back to Houston. Whatever you decide, Crys and I will be here to help you take care of everything, okay?"

I nodded against her chest, but I really couldn't even begin to think about anything at that moment, much less make life decisions. A little bit later Crys joined us in the embrace on the bed, and slowly Max, Andi, and Will all made their way in there as well. And there we all sat silently, all six of us on the bed holding each other, all six of lost in our thoughts of how we had lost such a vital person in our lives.

~   ~   ~   ~   ~

The following day we all went out to one of the beaches that he and I had frequented that summer. I had never met his dad before, and not surprisingly, he looked just like Ash but dressed in expensive clothes. The sky was gloomy gray which matched our moods just perfectly. Words were scarce; no one knew what to say. We walked down one of the jetties and his mom released his ashes over the choppy, dark blue water. One of the angry waves quickly crashed down on them, the ocean consuming what it had not previously taken. Silently, we all walked back to our cars. His dad didn't say a word to me the entire time. He got in his rental car and drove away without as much as saying goodbye to any of us. Crys muttered, "Asshole" under her breath, and Robin just hugged her in return.

I had returned to my state of numbness, I felt like I was walking around in a trance. None of it was sinking in, I kept thinking I was trapped in an awful nightmare, one that I just couldn't wake up from. Max had tried numerous times to comfort me, but I refused to talk to him. Hey kept telling me that he knew how I felt, that he had been there before, but I didn't want to talk about Evie's death any more than I wanted to talk about Ash's. That was just a reminder of all of the death that surrounded me.

CHAPTER TWENTY FOUR
Autumn Leaves ~ Ed Sheeran
Time of Our Lives ~ Tyrone Wells

SCARLETT

The odds of someone dying before there twenty-fifth birthday in America was roughly six percent, well that was the best I could determine from the thousands of results on Google. The odds of knowing two people that died before turning twenty five was a fraction of one percent. God either thought I had exceptional emotional and mental strength to be a part of that exclusive group or I was just fucking cursed, and my money was on the latter. I resolved to myself the day after Ash's ceremony that I would never fall in love again. I couldn't handle losing anyone else.

Max and Andi insisted that I return home with them, and I didn't really fight them on the issue. I didn't care enough to. Wherever I was, I'd just simply be existing. Robin and Crys seemed to think that was best idea too; no one wanted to leave me alone at the apartment. They said they'd box up all of our stuff and ship it back to me. I didn't understand how they could be so productive throughout everything. Didn't they realize they were never going to see their son and brother again? Like he was gone... vanished... no more.

Once we returned to Houston, I stayed in bed for about three weeks straight. I would nibble on the food that they would bring to me, but I had no appetite. I showered every four or five days, when I felt like it was absolutely necessary. Each time I would get out of the shower, I noticed that one of them would change my sheets. Mina and Jess both tried to come visit me, but I wouldn't see them. Max told me that he let Mason know because he was concerned that I wasn't replying to texts. I'm sure he wanted to stay as far away from me as possible, if he valued his life.

Finally, one day Max insisted I get up or he was going to call my parents. I hadn't even called them to tell them what happened and that I was home; as far as they were concerned, I was still playing house with Ash and lost in my music that would get me nowhere... I'm pretty sure those were their words the last time I talked to them. Reluctantly, I got out of bed and took a shower, just to put another pair of pajamas on. I made my way to the living room where I found a surprise visitor waiting for me ~ Heather.

I went to turn around and head back to my room, pissed off at them for bringing her here, when she grabbed me from behind and spun me around. She put her hand under my chin and tilted my face up to look in her eyes. "I'm not leaving here without you. Now go pack some clothes in a bag or I'll do it for you. Don't fight me on this, Scarlett," she said sternly.

I did as she told me to; I didn't have the fight in me to argue with her. A little while later I was checking in to the very place that I had been to visit while Mase was in rehab, wasn't that ironic? Heather helped me get situated in my room, and then told me that my first counseling session was immediately.

"Scarlett, let me tell you, that I have never gone and gotten someone from their home before and brought them here, but I'll be damned if I'm gonna allow a beautiful, vibrant young girl like yourself rot away because you were dealt a shitty hand in life. Bad things happen to good people. I know that you have the lost two people that you loved dearly in a very short amount of time. I know that you feel guilt for that, even though neither of their deaths had anything to do with you. I know that you feel like you like you never want to love again so that you never have to feel this hurt again. I know you probably don't care if you live to see tomorrow. I know all of those things, but I need you to listen to me and listen to me good." I just sat on the bed as she summed up my thoughts perfectly. "I also know that you are a smart and talented girl with a big heart, and there are a ton of people that are still here that don't want to lose you too. I've told you before that you've got to learn to love yourself. You've got to believe that, you, Scarlett, are worth being loved and your life is worth living, and I'm not going to let you leave here until I'm sure that you understand that."

~   ~   ~   ~   ~

Five months. That's roughly how long it took me to get Heather's message through my thick skull. Five month of straight counseling, both individual and group, on a daily basis and five months of unconditional love from my friends, no matter how ugly I was to them sometimes. Five months after I checked into The Right Step, I walked out with a glimmer of hope and belief that I would eventually be okay. I still had a lot of hurdles to jump, but I finally believed that I could maybe, just possibly, get over them.

The hardest thing for me to accept was that I really wasn't a curse to the ones I loved and I wasn't being punished for anything. As unreasonable as that may sound to some people, I couldn't help but think that there was some reason other than sheer coincidence that the two people that were closest to me died way before they should have. That took me a long time to accept, but once I did, it was easier for me to let go of the guilt.

Max, Andi, and Mina were relentless in their visits and they played a huge part in my recovery. One of them came up to see me almost every single day, and even at first when I would just sit there and not say a word, they just kept coming back. Once I began to come out of my protective shell a bit, Max brought me up my keyboard and my iPad so that I could reconnect with my music and start reading again, both of which helped save my sanity as well. I didn't realize how much I needed them in my life, but the outlet they provided me was vital for my mental health. Robin also visited me pretty regularly which made me feel good. She had told me that all of Ash and my stuff was in a storage unit and would stay right there until I was ready to go through it. Towards the end of my stay, I had finally gotten to where I could talk about happy memories with her. She told me about the time not too long ago when Ash had come over when she had a male friend stay the night. We both got a good laugh out of that.

Once I got home, I decided to sign up for some classes at the local community college for the spring semester. Rice wasn't allowing me to return after all of my coming-and-going over the previous two years, and quite honestly, I didn't think I could handle the stress of that level of academia at that point. I needed to take baby steps before I could run. I got a job teaching music classes to kids at the neighborhood center. It didn't pay well, but I really enjoyed it. Seeing the kid's faces as they began to really appreciate the music was priceless.

I hadn't heard from Mase since the night in Vegas. I knew that Max had told him about what happened to Ash, but I wasn't sure if he knew I was at the center or not. I would occasionally see pictures of him and the rest of the band in the entertainment magazines and websites. Apparently their tour was really successful and had been extended with the release of their second single. No one ever mentioned him to me, and to be honest, I was too afraid to ask. I assumed that he had just gotten too busy with everything to keep up with what was going on with crazy Scarlett. I'd be lying if I said it didn't hurt me, because it did ~ more so than I ever wanted to admit. I didn't understand how after everything he had said to me that day in Vegas, he could just drop me, but I guess fame really does change people.

I never went up to Empty's with Max and Andi because it just reminded me of him way too much, and I didn't need any hindrances. I was beginning to make some forward progress in my life, it was slow, but it was still progress. I still thought about Ash every day, and I missed him terribly. I missed Mase a lot too; we had become such good friends in addition to what we had shared before. I know a lot of people didn't understand how I could love them both, but I could... and I did. None of that mattered any longer though.

Just as Heather had always stressed, self-love was the greatest love. It was the only path to true happiness because in the end, if everyone else left, you had to be comfortable with just being you. I had thought that I was getting closer to that, but losing Ash, and subsequently Mase, caused a serious setback and forced me to realize that I still defined who I was by their existence. However, once on my own for a while, I began to realize that I was a good person with a lot to offer. Sure, I had made mistakes, who didn't? But I was trying hard to learn from those and to not repeat them. I loved sharing my musical talents, and as much as I had enjoyed performing with Max's band, getting the kids excited about music was so much more rewarding.

As for my love of books, it seemed that others enjoyed my reviews on *Ever Afters for Evie* because my followers continued to grow and I was getting great feedback on the letters. My intention was never for others to read them, but once I got a little following, I found that I greatly enjoyed talking about the books with fellow readers. One of the most important things I realized was that most everyone was searching for their happily ever after, in books and in real life, but that conclusion was always judged on if the girl got the guy in the end. It appeared I wasn't going to end up with either of my guys, but that didn't mean I couldn't be happy. I held the power that determined my own happiness.

CHAPTER TWENTY FIVE
Cover Your Tracks ~ A Boy and His Kite
Chasing Cars ~ Snow Patrol

SCARLETT

Book: When It Rains
Author: Lisa DeJung

Dear Evie,
As I'm writing you this letter, I am bawling... straight up, hard core bawling over the book I just finished. This is a cry that rivals Taking Chances, and unfortunately, my life, so I apologize in advance if I'm a babbling mess. This one's gonna be hard for me to review without giving away too much, and I REALLY want you to read this one, Evelyn Rose. As a matter of fact, I insist on it.
Where to begin, where to begin... ahhhh, my thoughts are all over the place! Okay, the main character of the story is Kate; she's a traumatized nineteen year old that is struggling to find her way back to the person that she used to be. She's got the amazing guy best friend, Beau, that has been there for her through thick and thin, and then she's got Asher, the guy that she feels an inexplicable connection with. (Yeah, you can imagine the goose bumps I got with that one ~ it may have hit a little too close to home.) The story really isn't a love triangle, even though it appears that way, but again I can't go too far into it without revealing the story. Did I mention you have to read this book? Ok, good.
So in addition to the impeccable writing and amazing flow to the book, the author does an incredible job of describing the ability to love two people and the different kinds of love that you can have. Seriously, it was like she got inside my heart and dug around all the feels that had been floating around for the last couple of years and put them into words. The story in itself is

beautifully heart-breaking and exquisitely gut-wrenching even without the personal connection that I made with it, but adding in that layer, it just sent me over the edge. I may need to take a break after this one before reading something else. It's got me all stirred up emotionally, and I'm really missing both Ash and Mase, as well as you... you know I'm always missing you. Until next time, I'll leave you with my favorite excerpt from the book, as I always do. Tell me how perfect this is... chill bumps from head to toe.
"I also realize that there's a difference between soul mates and true love. Looking at the surface, they are similar, but when I dug deep down inside, I found they were different." ~ Kate

Love you always,
Sam

Even in learning to love myself, I had learned that it was okay to miss the ones that I loved that were no longer around. It didn't mean that I was any less of a person on my own or that I was dependent on them for happiness. It simply meant that I loved them, and missed them being in my life ~ plain and simple.

MASON

The tour had finally come to an end. I never thought I'd say that, but damn if I wasn't ready to be home. Living on a tour bus for over half a year was about to drive me insane, especially knowing what Scarlett was going through back home. Once I had heard what happened to Ash, I was ready to bail on the tour, the band, everything. I didn't fucking care about any of that, but I allowed Max to talk me into giving her some time to process everything. He had said that the last thing she needed was me hovering over her and confusing her even more, and he warned me that she would probably lash out at me because she felt guilty that she was with me when the accident happened. I understood all of that. I didn't want to make things harder for her; all I wanted was to make sure my angel was okay. She had never left me in a time of need, and I didn't want her to think that I was abandoning her either.

I had called either Max or Andi to check on her every day. At first when they told me that she was spending a lot of time in bed and shutting herself off, I thought that was probably normal; however, when it began nearing a month, I started to freak out a bit. I couldn't stop thinking about her, and all I wanted was for her get better... I felt completely helpless thousands of miles away. When I called Heather and told her what had happened, she gave me her word that she would do everything in her power to bring my Scarlett back. Even if she was never my Scarlett again, I needed her to be okay for her.

Somehow, I managed to keep myself together for the band and the tour. It was my music that I poured my heart and soul into day after day that gave me the release and therapy to deal with what was going on. Every show that I did, every night that I went to bed, I saw as one day closer to getting to see her.

When the day came that I was flying into Houston to see her, I was more nervous than I had ever been in my life. I knew that she had been home for a few months and according to everyone, she was getting her life back on track. I didn't want my showing up to derail her in anyway, but at the same time, I couldn't go on living without telling her what was in my heart. She could do with it what she wanted; I would be at peace either way.

I pulled up to her apartment, taking several deep breaths before going in. As I walked up the front steps, I patted my pocket, ensuring that my gift for her was still in there, and then knocked on the door, waiting to see her beautiful face at least one more time. She answered the door and her jaw literally fell open as she stared at me.

"Angel," I whispered. My heart was pounding in my chest, my palms were clammy and sweaty, and my brain was moving so fast with so many things to tell her, that nothing else came out.

She smiled at me and tilted her head. "Mase, what are you doing here?"

"Well, we had our final show last night, so I got here as quick as I could," I said. "Do you care if I come in for a minute? I promise I won't take up much of your time."

She nodded and opened the door wider, allowing me to walk past her into the living room. I was too anxious to sit down, so I just stood by the bar as she shut the door. Turning around, my eyes caught hers and I prayed that I could get through my speech without breaking down. "Do you want to sit down? Can I get you something to drink?" she asked.

I shook my head no. "I'm good, thanks. I just wanted to come see you, to make sure that you were doing okay with my own two eyes. The secondhand reports for the last several months just weren't cutting it. I needed to know that the light had returned to your eyes."

"The secondhand reports? What are you talking about?"

A little confused, I explained, "Yes, the daily Scarlett reports I got from either Max or Andi. Did you not know that I called to check on you every day?"

"No, no, I didn't," she whispered.

"Ah, well, I did. I hope you don't mind, even though it's a little late now, I guess," I said with a chuckle.

"Wow, well I really appreciate it. I had no idea."

"I think your friends wanted to make sure that you got better, and they were afraid that I would try to get in the way of that." I shrugged. "All I wanted was for you to get better too." Damn, the speech was not going anything like I planned. She smiled at me, and I could see that she was unsure of what to say next, so I continued.

"Scarlett, I had this whole speech planned out before I got here, but the minute I saw your face, all other thoughts just escaped me. Basically, I'm here to tell you that I'm sorry about what happened to Ash. I know that it had nothing to do with me, but I'm sorry that it happened to him and I'm sorry that you had to deal with that. I know that he loved you dearly, as you did him, and regardless of my wishes for us to have worked out, my true priority has always been your happiness, even if it was him that gave you that.

I'm also here to tell you that my love for you has never wavered. I wanted you to know that I have followed your blog since the day you told me about it in a text message. I don't know much about any of those books, but reading your writing always helped me feel like I was still close to you, even when we weren't. I gotta tell you though; the one you wrote last week about the different kinds of love just about killed me, especially since you mentioned my name in it. I always *believed* that you had loved both of us, but it was hard for me to *understand* it. So I read the book, hoping that it would shed a little more light on it," I paused as my eyes began to water just thinking about both the letter and the book. "And all I can say is wow; that was the most intense thing I've ever read. I didn't know that a book could make me feel like that, and to be honest, I don't know how you made it through it. " She reached up and brushed her thumb across my upper cheek where a tear had escaped. I grabbed her hand and brought it to my mouth, kissing her open palm before releasing it. "But most importantly, I finally get it. I just wanted you to know that."

I stopped talking long enough to pull the box out of my pocket. "I don't know what the future holds for us, if anything at all, but I want you to have something to remind you that I will always love you." I heard her gasp for air as I opened the top and pulled out the contents. "I tried giving you this bracelet once before, but it didn't make it home with you. I think part of the reason was because it was incomplete. I hope now, it's perfect. Here, take a look"

She took the bracelet from my hands and began to examine it. She intensely studied it looking for what was different. She went through each of the dangling charms ~ the guitar, the piano, the heart, the book, the angel wings, and then she saw it. I wish I could describe the look on her face as she held the butterfly charm that I had added in her dainty fingers. The tears were streaming steadily down her cheeks but she had the biggest smile on her face. Then she turned it over and read the inscription on the back ~ "Psyche"

She flew into my arms and I held her as tightly as possibly could without hurting her. "I know that you'll always be his butterfly, and I never want you to forget that either. He and I were both lucky enough to be loved by someone as amazing as you, Angel. You now know that you don't need either of the wings that we adorned you with to fly on your own, but they're always here for you to remind you how much we both love you."

EPILOGUE ~ SIX YEARS LATER
Come to Me ~ Goo Goo Dolls

SCARLETT
One thing that I've learned about life in my short time here is that it never goes as planned. Learning to getting up each time that it knocks you down is hard; some of us get knocked down more than others, but in my opinion, we're the ones that are stronger in the end.

After Ash died, I truly thought that I'd never love anyone again. Even after I had come to terms with all of it and began to love myself for me, I didn't think that I could make myself susceptible to feeling pain like that again. But when Mase showed up on my door step that morning, all of that went out the window. I realized that loving yourself is vital because only then do you realize that you deserve the love of another.

I'd love to say that he walked in that day, swept me off my feet again, and we rode off into the sunset happily ever after, but that isn't reality, and actually it isn't even the ending of most books anymore.

"Mommy, Auntie Andi says it's time for us to get married," a sweet, tiny voice interrupted my thoughts.

I turned around to see my precious daughter standing in the doorway, dressed in her light pink sundress and flip flops. Laughing, I walked over to her and picked her up. "Did Auntie Andi say that you can get married in those shoes?" She nodded her head with a big grin on her face. "Well, in that case, I'm wearing my flip flops too. You don't think Daddy will mind do you?"

"No, Daddy and Everett have on their new black chucks. He said you'd like them," she said with a giggle.

I rolled my eyes as I sat Ashlynn down on the ground. "I don't care what they wear, as long as we all get to get married." I bent down to kiss the top of her head. "Now go tell Auntie Andi that mommy will be there in five minutes."

As she took off down the hallway, I turned around to look at myself one last time in the mirror and took a deep breath. Mase and I didn't get to this point the conventional way, and I wouldn't necessarily recommend it to anyone else, but it was how our book had to be written in order to get the ending just right. God really doesn't give us anything we can't handle, and what he takes away, he repays tenfold. Not a year after Mase and I rekindled our relationship, I ended up pregnant with twins. Even though no one or nothing could ever replace Evie and Ash, I was gifted two beautiful souls that taught me about even a different kind of love than I had already experienced. Now, finally, after three world tours and two babies, Mase and I, along with with Ashlynn and Everett, were going to be one complete family.

The wedding ceremony was perfect, even with Ashlynn announcing she had to pee in the middle of the vows, and the reception was even better. I couldn't stop smiling as I saw our friends and family eating, dancing, and having an overall great time. As the evening came to an end, Mase came up to me and grabbed my hand. "I've got a surprise for you."

He led me and all of the guests outside, then walked over to the event coordinator and whispered something in her ear. Returning to me, he stood behind me and circled his arms around my waist, pulling my back close to his chest. A song began playing through the outside speakers and he started singing lowly into my ear, then all of a sudden, the sky filled with butterflies... thousands of them. I stood there in complete awe, looking up into the heavens as the beautiful creatures blanketed the sky. He continued his serenade "Come to me my sweetest friend, this is where we start again..." When the song was over, he turned me around in his arms and pressed his forehead to mine. "Scarlett Alexandria Templeton, I have finally found my euphoria."

"Give the ones you love wings to fly, roots to come back, and reasons to stay." ~Dalai Lama

The End

Acknowledgements

A huge thank you to my family for their continued support throughout this entire year as I've embarked on this journey that I never planned on taking, especially my husband and my girls who have had to deal with my hours upon hours of time spent in the cave. They keep a smile on my face and remind me of why I am doing this. I love you all so very much.

Jennifer, Kiersten, and Trina ~ You ladies are amazing. I can't thank you enough for the time that you spent helping me with this book, your feedback and support are priceless.

Tracey ~ My Lenora. I love you, sissy. Thank you from the bottom of my heart.

Hang Le and Toski Covey ~ for an amazing cover, yet again. Bless your hearts.

The real life Heather ~ you are more of an inspiration than you could possibly know. I can't wait to read one of your books in print one day soon. You bring a new definition to evil...

My C and Drea ~ unicorn lovers unite forever, girlies. Thank you for keeping me sane and giving me an outlet to bitch and moan, but most importantly for being awesome friends.

Robin ~ my personal DJ ~ thank you for providing the music that helped inspire so much of this writing and being a great friend

The bloggers ~ thank you for all the time that you put into reading and reviewing these babies of ours, you're the reason that I can continue to do this

Check out these upcoming books from new indie authors in 2014:

The Promise ~ S. L. Jayne
Prologue
14 years ago- July 1999

"Goodnight, Avaloo, I love you more than the stars."

I giggled at the nickname she calls me when she is in a happy mood.

"Goodnight, Mommy. I love you lots and lots too, more than the stars."

After putting the story book down on my nightstand my mom tucked me into bed and kissed me on the forehead. It was the same routine every night. My bed time was 7:30pm, mom would dedicate thirty minutes to me so we could have our one on one time.

The sound of crying jolted me from my sleep, I sat up in my bed and listened. I glanced at the clock on my nightstand, it read 9:35pm. Who could be crying? I thought to myself. We live on a quiet street and our houses are close together, so if I can hear it why can't anybody else? I got up from my bed and walked across my room to the window. I couldn't see anybody out there. As I turned to make my way back to bed I saw her stand up, I rushed to open the window.

"Rylee? What are you doing out here this late? Why are you crying? What's wrong? What has happened?" I said panicking, I couldn't stop the questions flying out.

I had a feeling it was something to do with her step dad Nate, but I didn't want to mention him and upset her more. She looked at me with tears streaming down her face. She dropped her head, her voice was shaking.

"I had to get out of there, Ava. I hate him. Can I come in? Please." she whispered.

"Yes, get in here, what's wrong, Rylee? We will have to be quiet so my mom doesn't hear us though."

I helped her through the window and we settled on my bed. I have so many questions right now. I want to ask her what has happened but I know she just needs a friend to listen and not ask questions right now. Sitting with my back against my headboard Rylee lays her head in my lap facing the window and I stroke her hair.

"Take deep breaths, Rylee. You don't have to tell me right now what has happened but this time is different, all the other times that you have been upset you haven't gone against the rules and left the house. Is it that bad?" I said in a hushed voice.

She takes a deep breath and I hear her breathing even out and she nods her head.

"He told me I spend too much time with my mom when I shouldn't because she loves him and Connor more than me." She said through a jagged breath.

A mixture of feelings are rushing through me in this moment. Shock, sympathy, anger, hurt. All for my best friend, the one that is so sweet and funny and caring. How could somebody say something so cruel to her?

"That isn't true, Rylee. He is lying. Your mom loves you and Conner the same, she loves spending time with you. You need to tell your mom what he has said, or we can tell my mom? We can do it together, you won't be alone."

She really needs to tell an adult what is happening, she has told her mom things before but they were different things, things like when he bought Conner more candy than her or when they went shopping and Conner got a new toy but she didn't. Those things her mom overlooked and said it is because he is younger and doesn't understand the word *no* just yet. She looked up at me shaking her head.

"No, Ava. I don't want to tell anyone. My mom will think I'm being silly and that will make him happy knowing my mom thinks that." She crinkled her nose. "And I don't want to do anything that will make *him* happy."

I giggled at her looking mean and nodded.

"Okay. We'll do whatever you want, whenever you're ready." I smiled. "Don't forget my birthday is in one week so you will get a night away from him. I can't wait, my sleepover is going to be so much fun."

She got up off the bed and started walking towards the window, I followed her so I could close it when she left.

Turning to face me she said. "I know I can't wait, I hope Nate says I can come."

"Thank you for letting me come in." She smiled big. "I couldn't ask for a better best friend. Even if God sent me an angel I don't think she would be better than you. We'll be best friends forever and ever."

My face broke into the biggest smile and I hugged her tight.

"Aw, Rylee. You are the bestest friend anyone could ask for, we will definitely be best friends forever. Anyway, you know who my crush is so I have to be nice to you so you don't tell him." She burst out laughing.

"Shhhh!" I reminded her that we needed to be quiet.

"Oops, sorry!" She lowered her voice but it was still slightly high pitched. "You had to make me laugh, but I do feel better now that I have laughed. Thank you. Oh and don't worry, your secret crush on Ryan Sanders is safe with me."

She giggled as she climbed out of the window and made her way across the grass to her house. I could throw a stone and it would land in her backyard, that's how close our houses are. I saw her stop half way.

"I won't tell him that you *always* talk about him on our movie nights and how perfect you think his hair is." She said over her shoulder and ran the rest of the way before I could say anything.

***

I woke up on my birthday morning to my mom walking into my bedroom singing happy birthday to me.

"Happy birthday, Avaloo. Daddy is downstairs cooking your favorite breakfast." She handed me the small box that is wrapped in bright pink paper with a small bow on top. I sat up quickly in my excitement and smiled up at her.

"Thank you, Mom. I'm going to love it, whatever it is!" I said as I ripped the paper off and opened the box.

I gasped when I saw it, there were two silver necklaces with a love heart pendent hanging on each chain. It was one of those necklaces that Rylee and I had talked about on one of our movie nights, the kind that when the two halves were put together it said *best friends*, we wanted one so bad. I hope she is allowed to come tonight, it won't feel the same without her. I climbed out of bed and gave my mom a big hug.

"WOW! Thank you, Mom. Thank you so much, I love it! I can't wait to show Rylee and to give her the other half." My face was hurting from smiling so big.

"You're welcome, sweetie. I'm glad you like it and I'm sure Rylee will love to have the other half." She smiled back at me. "Now let's go and eat pancakes and get the rest of your presents."

The day went really fast, mom and I decorated my room with balloons and banners and now I am all ready for my friends. I'm keeping my fingers crossed that Rylee comes. I hear the doorbell chime and I make my way to the door. Lillie- Mai and Hanna have arrived together. I was so happy to see them.

"Hi! Come in. We have candy, soda, movies and make-up. It's going to be so much fun!" My words come out *sooo* fast, it always happens when I'm excited. I took them into the living room, we sat down while my mom got our drinks.

"Rylee should be here soon." As soon as I finished my sentence there was a knock on the door.

I jumped up and ran to answer it, hoping it was Rylee. I opened the door and jumped up and down when I saw her standing there. "YES, you came! I'm so glad you're here. Come in, Lillie-Mai and Hanna are here too." She gave me a huge smile.

"My mom said I could come, I'm so happy right now!"

It was getting late and Lillie-Mai had already giggled herself to sleep. We had watched a movie, had makeovers, ate lots of chips and candy, and were hyper on soda. We laughed until our tummy's hurt while we talked about boys, being famous, and our favorite boy bands. Hanna was the next to fall asleep leaving Rylee and I awake, we lay in my bed together talking about our future plans. Rylee was telling me her thoughts.

"We should live in California and we can get famous boyfriends and have a double wedding!"

I laughed. "Yeah, great idea, Ry. We can share an apartment and go to the beach and shopping trips and then eat all the ice cream we want while we watch movies."

She turned and smiled at me. "Have you had a good birthday?"

I nodded my head fast, "I've had a great birthday. I've had so much fun! Oh, wait. I have a surprise for you."

She looked at me and frowned. "For me? But it's *your* birthday, Ava."

I giggled. "Yes, for you. I know it's my birthday and this is part of my birthday. Close your eyes and hold out your hand." I took the necklace out of the box and placed it in her palm. "Open now!" Rylee opened her eyes and stared at the necklace.

"Oh my gosh, Ava! Is this one of those necklaces?"

I nodded at her, knowing exactly what kind she thought. I helped her put it on, "Now we really are the bestest of friends." When Rylee turned around to face me I could see her eyes filling up with tears.

"What's wrong, Rylee?" She stepped towards me and hugged me.

"I want to move away, Ava. As soon as we are old enough, I want to get away from *him* and all of his nastiness. Please say you will come with me? Please. We can move to California, as soon as we are done with college. Please, Ava." She was begging me to say yes.

What could have been said to her that would make her hate

Nate so bad? I wish she would tell me what's happened.

"Okay, I'll come with you. We'll move out of Boston and make a new life in California." I said as I nodded at her.

She stared at me with her eyes wide open. "Really? No questions asked, you're really going to move away with me?"

I nodded "Yeah, Rylee. No questions asked. I'm there."

She looked at me with serious eyes. "Pinky promise?"

I smiled back at her, knowing what this promise means to us both. We only pinky promise on things we will never break. I will make sure I get my best friend far away from here one day. I held out my pinky finger and she hooked hers around mine.

"Pinky Promise."

New Beginnings
By: S.N. Williams
Estimated Release Date: Middle of January 2014

Laying there I hear people talking but can't seem to open my eyes. What's wrong with me? Why can't I talk? What the hell happened to me? Did I die? Why can't I open my eyes? I am starting to freak out then I hear beeping in the distance. It sounds like a heart monitor. That has to be my heart right? It's eratic. Am I in the hospital? How did that happen? I can't remember anything happening. I keep hearing myself scream hoping they hear me. I try to move my legs and they feel as they way a ton. I try my arms next, with the same feeling of being weighed down. I hear the door open and hear two people come in through the door. Finally someone heard me. I hear them saying something about how lucky I was to still be alive. I hear whoever it is talking that they had to put me into an induced coma. Coma. I am in a coma. They continue to talk saying it was necessary with my brain swelling. I feel one of them pulling at something in my arm. I feel liquid going through my vein in my hand. I scream again. They can't hear me. All my screaming was in my head. I hear the door open and they are gone. What the hell happened? I need to know what is going on. I need my husband. Not being able to hold on any longer I see darkness coming. I am dying right? Then I am gone.

Made in the USA
San Bernardino, CA
09 January 2014